Shannon stopped thinking…

His lips. Her lips. Tog... ...ing. *Oh.*

Thinking would come later. Now was for goose bumps and heat. She'd wanted this so much…it was definitely in the cards.

Nate's right hand floated near her face before his fingertips brushed the path of her blush up her cheek to her temple. "You're so beautiful," he said, then winced slightly. "More than beautiful. How did that happen? When?"

"You went away."

"And you became a gorgeous woman."

She doubted she could blush harder. "You came back better, too."

"Older, at least." His fingers moved into her hair, carefully, slowly. "Hopefully wiser."

"Definitely better," she said, momentarily panicked that wiser meant he knew they shouldn't be doing this.

"I don't want to stop."

She stepped closer to him, letting more of her body press against his.

"No one's asking you to…."

Dear Reader,

Welcome to the final story in the It's Trading Men! trilogy. Writing these three books (*Choose Me, Have Me* and *Want Me*) has been fun. I've fallen in love with Charlie, Jake and Nate, and want to be like Bree, Rebecca and Shannon.

Shannon Fitzgerald came up with the brilliant notion of using trading cards to trade men. You'd think she would have been the first to find her Mr. Right. *Wrong!*

Fiery redhead Shannon has more than the St. Marks lunch exchange on her mind. She's doing everything in her power to keep her family's business afloat, she's coordinating a huge Easter fundraiser and she's giving up hope that she'll ever find true love. When she runs into long-time family friend Nate Brenner at a wedding, she immediately sees his potential as a trading card hottie.

The last thing either Shannon or Nate imagines is for sparks to fly between them. Especially since Nate is sharing Shannon's house…in the bedroom next door! When sparks turn into a passionate flame, both of their lives are changed forever…especially when the trading cards for trading men become a national scandal, with Nate and Shannon in the heart of the storm!

As always, I can be reached at joleigh@joleigh.com, and hearing from readers is the best thing ever!

Love to you all,

Jo Leigh

Jo Leigh

WANT ME

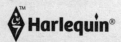

Harlequin®

TORONTO NEW YORK LONDON
AMSTERDAM PARIS SYDNEY HAMBURG
STOCKHOLM ATHENS TOKYO MILAN MADRID
PRAGUE WARSAW BUDAPEST AUCKLAND

Recycling programs
for this product may
not exist in your area.

ISBN-13: 978-0-373-79681-6

WANT ME

www.Harlequin.com

Printed in U.S.A.

ABOUT THE AUTHOR

Jo Leigh is from Los Angeles and always thought she'd end up living in Manhattan. So how did she end up in Utah, in a tiny town with a terrible internet connection, being bossed around by a house full of rescued cats and dogs? What the heck, she says, predictability is boring. Jo has written more than forty novels for Harlequin Books. She can be contacted at joleigh@joleigh.com.

Books by Jo Leigh

HARLEQUIN BLAZE

To get the inside scoop on Harlequin Blaze and its talented writers, be sure to check out blazeauthors.com.

As always,
I owe so many thanks to Debbi and Birgit
for being true partners
in this crazy writing endeavor.

1

THE WEDDING WAS IN FULL swing, "The Irish Rover" was in heavy rotation by the band, beer was flowing and the hundred and fifty friends and family of Theresa O'Brian-Moran were halfway to hangovers.

Shannon Fitzgerald had found a relatively quiet corner. It had taken Shannon the better part of the evening to convince herself to approach her second cousin about joining the small and exclusive St. Marks lunch exchange. But Ariel was perfect, really. At twenty-four, she was three years younger than Shannon, lived in Nolita, worked in Midtown and was still single, as was Shannon. Arial was also very pretty and had attracted a group of red-faced, very happy young men wanting to dance.

Shannon had pulled in her share of slightly older young men, mostly in the twenty-eight-to-thirty-five range, although Angus was hovering and he'd just turned eighty-three. It was like being caught in a swarm of bees. Shannon and Ariel kept swatting them away, but they just circled over to the bar, then came back.

"Trading cards?" Ariel asked, leaning in so she'd be heard above the fiddles and tin whistle of the band and the tipsy pleading of brokenhearted boys. "I thought it was a lunch exchange."

Shannon nodded. "It's both. If you want to do the food part, you bring in frozen lunches for fourteen, then you take home your own fourteen lunches. It saves a ton of money and gives you variety, but the important thing is the trading cards. All of us have friends or exes or coworkers who are eligible single men."

She pushed her cousin Riley a full arm's length away without giving him a glance. His breath. God. "Nice men," Shannon continued. "Men we'd want our best friend to go out with."

Ariel nodded slowly, fussing a little with the bodice of her pink dress, then her eyes lit up. "David Sainsbury at my office. He's off-limits to me, but he's extremely nice and he just broke up with his girlfriend. He'd be a real catch. He's always nice to the temps, and he gets coffee for his assistant every time he gets a cup for himself. He's funny, too."

"There you go," Shannon said, tickled about the addition of David, who sounded like someone she might be interested in.

"How do I do this? Submit his name?"

"You procure a picture of David, a head shot is best, let us see what we're getting. I'll make sure you have a few samples of the cards that are no longer in circulation. Then I put the picture on the front of the trading card."

"Oh, yes. Of course. The printing plant."

Shannon wondered if that was Ariel's first beer. Fitzgerald & Sons was a huge part of the extended family. Ariel's father had worked there for over ten years before he opened his stationery store. But then it was hard to think in all this craziness. "For the back of the card," Shannon said, deciding right then to reiterate all of this information in a follow-up email, "you fill out a short form. It starts with his profession. Then whether he's a marry, date or one-night stand."

Ariel's head tilted as she let the second part sink in. "Ah," she said, when the beauty of that key piece of information hit.

"Exactly. Next, his favorite restaurant. Then his secret passion. Not his career but the thing he loves more than anything. Sports or movies or dancing. Whatever turns him on."

"David is completely into science fiction. He's always got a book nearby."

The wistfulness of Ariel's voice made it clear that Shannon wouldn't be going out with David. She and Ariel were cousins, and she wasn't interested in starting a family feud. "Are you sure he's off-limits?"

"Company policy. He's one of their top attorneys."

"Maybe it'd be worth it to try and find another job," Shannon said, turning briefly to shoo away one of the Wilson twins.

Ariel shook her head. "I've put out feelers. It's murder out there. I'm not risking my job for anything. They have full medical."

"Understood." She took a sip of her white wine, sacrilege in this crowd, but Shannon didn't care. Beer was for the pub. Wine was for weddings. "After his passion comes the bottom line—what it is that makes him special. Why you're recommending him. Then, I put that information on the back of the card, do the printing and, voilà, we have Hot Guys Trading Cards."

"I love this idea," Ariel said. "I really do."

"It works. It's safe, too, because the person who submits the card sets up the date. And no one outside the group knows the cards exist."

"Including the guys?"

"Especially the guys." Shannon made a point of looking Ariel in the eyes. "The whole thing is a secret, very private. No one knows outside the group. Understand?"

Ariel nodded, took a healthy swig of her beer and grinned, showing off her expensive dental work. "It's brilliant."

"I know," Shannon said, not even a little bit embarrassed to say so since the whole concept had been her idea. "We've only been swapping cards for a couple of months, and it's exceeded our expectations. The only problem we haven't solved is how to keep increasing the dating pool while still keeping it a secret. Very tricky."

"Shannon." The deep voice behind her made her look because she couldn't immediately identify who was speaking. It wasn't a cousin, which was astonishing, but he might as well have been. "Hello, Mike."

"I was wondering if you'd like to take a turn with me?" He nodded toward the dance floor.

Mike was a nice man, almost thirty, owned a bookstore that was holding on by a thread, and she felt guilty for not liking him more. They'd tried dating once and there'd been no chemistry whatsoever. Maybe she should put him on a card. He really was sweet. "Oh, sorry. Maybe later? I'm in the middle."

"Sure, sure thing," Mike said, giving her a dejected smile. "I'll be around."

As soon as he was out of earshot, which was a matter of two steps, Ariel leaned in again. "What kind of men are on the cards? Are there any restrictions?"

"Nope. Except that they need to be local. And looking. There've already been some epic matches. Like Charlie Winslow and Bree Kingston."

Ariel's jaw dropped. "That was you?"

Shannon smiled. "It was."

"Holy cow. That's incredible. I'm in."

"Great." Shannon pulled out a tiny little notepad that fit in her tiny bridesmaid's purse that matched her pale green dress perfectly. "I'll give you the address and—"

Ariel was no longer listening. She was staring over Shannon's shoulder. "Is he on a card?"

Shannon looked where Ariel was pointing. "Danny? No. I decided not to put my brothers into the mix. Too complicated. Besides, since when have you been interested in—"

"Not Danny, the guy with Danny."

The guy in question looked kind of familiar. His body, on the other hand…

"What? Who is he? Do you know him?"

"No, I don't think so. I'd remember," she murmured as she checked out his shoulder-to-waist ratio, which looked to be perfect. He was in a white oxford shirt, top button undone, dark tie loosened. His slacks were a great fit, designer, not off-the-rack. The whole package was hot. His dark hair, the way he tilted his head back as he laughed, his smile…

"Oh, my God." Shannon stood up, stuffed the unfinished note back in her bag. "That's Nate Brenner."

"Who?"

"Danny's friend. I haven't seen him in ages."

"Well, go find out if he's single, would you? He's a total babe."

Shannon nodded as she headed his way, staring hard to make sure she was right. Yep. The closer she got, the clearer it became that the boy who'd practically grown up with her family was not a boy anymore. How had that happened? Time, of course, but because she hadn't seen him in so long, he'd continued to be eighteen and skinny and more than a little obnoxious to the thirteen-year-old sister of his best friend. No more obnoxious than her own brothers, though. All four had been insufferable. They'd made fun of her hair, of her desire to be on the stage. It hadn't helped that they'd been forced to come to the various pageants where she'd posed and danced and belted out her off-key songs. She'd made them miss games. The unforgivable sin.

When it came to her four older siblings every topic of conversation was centered on sports. *Every* conversation. Even when the discussion was about, say, books, they were sports books. Movies—sports. Okay, that and car crashes, but those were sports films in a way. Women entered the picture only if they first passed the team test. If they were crazy about Notre Dame football, they were in. The Yankees? In. The only variable was the Boston Celtics. They weren't the favorite, but they were acceptable.

She'd suspected there was more to Nate; he'd been more pensive, more intense than her hooligan brothers, but she'd been young when he disappeared, so she'd stopped wondering.

The transition from teenager to man had been very, very good to Nate, that was for sure. He would be thirty-two now, same as Danny. She'd never once thought of him as being good-looking. Passable, yes, cute, maybe. But hot? Not a chance.

"Hey, Princess," Danny said, as she got within talking distance. "Look who's here."

Nate's eyebrows lifted and his smile widened. "That can't be Shannon."

"It can and it is," she said, and then they were hugging, and it felt weird as hell for a whole list of reasons. His chest, for one thing. Firm, strong, broad. The feel of her breasts against it was sparking things that she had no business even noticing. This was a guy she'd known since she could remember. She'd seen him in his Spider-Man pajamas. They'd been his favorites, although sometimes he'd worn a cape or carried a light saber.

She pulled back to look at him. "Where the *hell* have you been? It's been forever."

"All over the place. It's too long a story to bore you with now. I want to hear what you've been doing." He looked her over then did the vertical version of a double take. "Aside from...you're all grown up."

"That tends to happen," she said. "So are you."

"I'll admit I got older. But I'm not sure about the grown-up part."

"Do you still put cherry bombs in toilets?"

He and Danny cracked up. "No," Nate said. "I'm very proud to say that I stopped doing that."

"It's a start," she said. "Did you come back for the wedding?"

"Coincidence. I've got business. Selling my father's firm. And looking for a town house."

"Selling your father's... Oh, God. I heard about your dad. I'm so sorry." He'd passed away two years ago, and she'd meant to write Nate.

"Thanks," he said as if it were nothing, but then his jaw tensed.

Shannon wouldn't have noticed if she hadn't been staring so rudely. "Did something happen to your house in Gramercy?"

"My mom sold it. She's living in Tel Aviv now. Got remarried. She's working at the university there."

"That's quite a few major changes."

"Not really. You Fitzgeralds are amazingly stable, that's all. What, it's only you and Brady still living in that huge brownstone?"

"And the parents."

"Uh, sorry to interrupt," Danny said. "I'm going to see if I can get Megan to dance with me." He poked Nate in the chest. "You can tell the Princess here all about your adventures. And the good news."

Shannon watched her brother dive into the heart of the crowd.

"So they still call you 'Princess'?"

She looked back at Nate with a sigh. "I've given up trying to make them stop. They're horrible, all of them. I can't imagine why you still like Danny."

Nate touched the back of her arm, and it jolted her like a static charge. "Every one of your brothers would throw themselves on a sword for you."

"When?" she asked.

He laughed, and it was so much deeper than when he'd been eighteen. She looked at him again. "How's your sister?"

"Married. With a kid. A little girl. They live in Montauk."

"Good for her."

Nate looked at the dance floor, his hand still on her arm. "You want to give it a go?"

She hadn't danced yet, and since the set was now modern music instead of traditional Irish dance, she smiled. "I'd love to." Nodding at a beer mug on the closest table, she said, "Your table?"

He slipped her purse from her fingers and put it next

to the mug. "It is now." Then he led her to a corner where they had some chance of not getting an elbow in the ribs.

Shannon liked the song, although she never gave it a thought outside of weddings or elevators, but the beat was good, and she was feeling fine. Happy. She'd recruited Ariel, been completely surprised by Nate and no one had asked her to sing or do any step dancing. It had been part of her repertoire as a young girl, but she'd let it go when she entered high school. Sadly, the family hadn't.

She moved to the music, got her rhythm then smiled at Nate. Ten seconds later, it was all she could do not to burst out laughing.

He was *awful.* The kind of awful that had to be genetic because no one would choose to dance that way. None of his limbs seemed connected to any of his other limbs, and what was he doing with his *head?*

She squeaked as she held her smile in place, and he was grinning right back at her as if he owned the whole dance floor.

Danny and Megan swung close by and Danny, her complete ass of a brother, slugged Nate in the shoulder, laughing so hard he had to stop everything else. "You are the saddest excuse for a white guy I have ever seen on a dance floor. Jesus, Nate, you look like someone stuck a firecracker up your ass."

Nate grinned at Danny and kept on doing…whatever it was he was doing. "I am my own man in every way," he said—no, shouted—then he spun around in an oval. "You don't recognize true artistic expression, you heathen. Be gone." He flapped his hand, although it was pretty much what he was doing already.

She laughed. But not because he was a total dork.

Because he embraced being a dork. Her hand, she noticed, was over her heart, and despite the music and the utter chaos around her, all she could think was that Nate hadn't just grown into a really good-looking man, he'd also become completely adorable.

The music stopped, but only for a second, and the next song was faster, wilder, and she let go. By God, she let herself dance as if she were in her bedroom, as if no one were watching. Like Nate.

His laughter hit her as she spun around, and she couldn't help returning it. They'd earned themselves a nice slice of dance floor, and she couldn't remember the last time she'd felt so free. The song ended too soon, and the two of them fell together to gasp in some much-needed breath.

"That was fantastic," he said.

"It was."

"Not a lot of women appreciate my unique style."

"They're fools and cretins."

"Ah, Shannon. You're too kind."

"Oh, I'm not. I'm really, really not."

Another song started, but this one was a slow tune, a romantic number that made her wonder if she should beg off, or…

He slipped his arms around her waist and started moving. Nothing fabulous, but also nothing uniquely styled. She found it easy to put her hands on his shoulders, to let her heartbeat slow.

"Adventures, huh?"

He shook his head a little. Met her gaze. "Of a sort."

"Danny mentioned you'd gone to help out after the Indonesian tsunami."

Nate nodded. "I did. I had skills, they needed help."

"And now?"

"They still need it. A lot of people do. I work for an organization that sends me where I can do some good."

Someone bumped her from behind, pushing her against Nate's body from knee to chest. Her first instinct was to put space between them, but there was also something else going on that wasn't the crowd and certainly wasn't dancing. There was no way not to look at him, and he was watching her as if they were alone in the room. He'd felt the tension, that was clear. A frisson went through her, and he felt that, too.

Another bump, but this one parted them the way she hadn't been able to.

He swallowed, glanced around at the crowd, then back at her. "I could use a drink after all that self-expression. Do you mind? Our table's open. I can get us drinks."

Thank goodness. She had no idea what the hell was up with those last few moments and she needed some space to get her breath back. "Great. White wine for me, please."

"Rebel."

She grinned. "That's me."

He walked her to the table and her smile faded as she watched him make his way to the bar. If he'd been anyone else, she'd have known what all that sizzle and smoke had been about. Any other guy. Part of her wanted to apologize and assure him she hadn't meant to press against him so intimately. But since she had… No. That wasn't at all what she wanted to tell him. She had no idea what she wanted to say. Mostly because she hadn't been able to read him. For a moment, she'd thought… But that was ridiculous.

He'd been a hellion as a kid. Forever taking risks, talking big. It had gotten him into a lot of messes, and he'd dragged Danny along for most of those, but he'd always been welcome in the Fitzgerald home. Especially since his folks had worked such long hours.

She had to wonder if he were still reckless, ready to jump into crazy situations without a second thought. His work sounded like something to be proud of, but also dangerous. Although she had to consider she'd known only the boy, not the man. Fourteen years was a long time, and she sure wasn't the girl she'd been back then. Or maybe she was. It was sometimes hard to tell.

While he was out of sight, she freshened her lipstick, practically the only thing she'd had room for in her purse aside from the small pen and notepad, a twenty and breath mints. Stupid little thing. At least the brides-maid's dress was nice. Not great, just a simple sleeve-less sheath with a sweetheart neckline. In the past year alone, Shannon had been forced to wear five dresses that would never see the light of day again. At least this time she hadn't been the maid of honor.

She suspected all her friends and relatives asked her because of her connections. Being in charge of sales and marketing for the printing plant meant she was on a first-name basis with almost every vendor from Chelsea all the way down to the Village.

"What's that scowl about?"

Nate put down her glass as well as his big mug of beer, then sat across from her. It caused a stir inside her that was frankly inappropriate. Good grief, she had to get over this. What she should be excited about was putting him on a trading card. A man with his looks, his international lifestyle, his unforgettable dancing needed to be out there. And the good women of St. Marks lunch exchange needed a breath of fresh air.

He'd had a good haircut. Not overstyled, but neat.

Whoever had had him on the chair understood that his high forehead was an asset, and that he could carry a longer sideburn than most.

"You're good-looking," she said. Then froze. She hadn't meant to say that out loud.

Grabbing his beer, he paused. "What's that?"

Oh, what the hell. She was busy, he was busy, after tonight she probably wouldn't see him again for another ten years. "You. I thought you were okay when you were in high school, but now you're actually handsome."

He fought a smile for a long minute. "Thank you?"

"You're welcome. Now, what was the good news you were supposed to tell me?"

"I'm moving in. With you."

2

NATE WATCHED HER EXPRESSION change from surprise to greater surprise. He sipped his beer to hide his grin.

"Oh?" she said, sounding as disinterested as a person who absolutely wasn't.

He nodded. "I was staying at Hotel Giraffe, but your mom had a fit, so now I'm moving in tomorrow."

"Danny's, Myles's or Tim's?"

He huffed out a laugh. "You think I'd risk my life in anyone's but Myles's room? Your brothers are savages."

She'd gotten herself under control, which was a pity. At least, her exterior was collected as could be, but he wondered. That dance… Not the first two, because he was under no illusions that he looked anything but preposterous attempting to move to music. Luckily for him, he'd quit worrying. He had other good qualities. Besides, if someone didn't like it they could piss right off.

He was actually thinking of the slow dance, the one where he'd felt her breasts against his chest. The one he'd had to cut short in case she felt his reaction.

There it was. The big deal, the shock, the bewildering new reality. Shannon had grown up to be an absolute stunner. She'd been a gorgeous kid, so why it was such a surprise wasn't clear, but he doubted anyone could have guessed she'd turn into the goddamn Venus on the Half Shell.

It started with her hair. Thick and past her shoulders, it was a lush, fiery red-orange wonder. Especially when she used both hands to sweep it off her neck before letting it fall.

"There's plenty of room at the house these days," she said. "How long will you be in residence?"

They'd been talking. He'd forgotten. "I'm supposed to be back in Bali by the middle of May. But I'm hoping to wrap things up here sooner than that."

"Oh. I thought you were looking to buy a town house."

"I am," he said, keeping his gaze straight ahead so he didn't get derailed again. "Mostly because I need the expenses to offset my capital gains. I'll sublet the place, but first I have to find something, then furnish it." He exhaled, happy that he'd found a topic so boring that his still-too-interested cock would settle in for the night.

Shit, the feeling of her in his arms revisited, and so much for boring capital-gains talk. She'd been a straight-as-a-board kid when he'd moved to his place at New York University, thirteen and a complete drama queen. Every time she spoke it was life or death, where she was the center of the universe, and none of her brothers had much patience. Especially when she kept popping up when he and Danny had convinced girls that they wouldn't be caught sneaking into the house after ten because Mom and Dad Fitzgerald's bedroom was on the third floor and they slept like the dead.

"In Gramercy?"

He had no idea why she'd asked… Oh. "I don't care where it is. Or what. Duplex, town house, row house, apartment. It needs to be in Manhattan, needs to be managed so that I can be gone most of the year without worrying, and it would be nice if it brought in some decent money. If you have any ideas or know of anything, that would be great."

"I'll ask around."

"Thanks." He picked up his beer again, she lifted her wine, and then she turned to look out at the dance floor and his shoulders sagged in relief.

This was Shannon. Little Shannon. He'd known her since he was eight, and she'd been a pest for the next ten years. But now she had curves and legs that went all the way down to the ground, perfect white teeth and deep green eyes. For a natural redhead, she had fewer freckles than he would have imagined, and oh, God, she was a natural redhead, which meant that all her hair was—

"I might know of something in the Flatiron District, come to think of it," she said, and she was looking at him again.

Great. He refused to even acknowledge the jerk in his crotch because he was thirty-two and Shannon had practically been his sister back in the day. "Hey," he said, leaning over the table, focusing, "you were always redecorating your room."

Shannon laughed. "I was a teenage girl. That wasn't decorating, that was illustrating. I was constantly falling madly in love with movie stars or deeply wounded singers."

"Your bedroom always looked nice. Smelled great, too."

"Yes, because I wasn't a savage who left my unwashed gym clothes to stew on the floor for months."

"Oh." Nate leaned back. "That actually makes sense. We were pigs, weren't we?"

She gave him an eye-roll. "I gather you want some assistance with the furnishings?"

He shook his head. "More than that. I need someone to help me find the right place, then furnish it. A woman's touch would be welcome. I've been building basic housing for a long time, living in tents or huts. I don't know the market at all. But I can hire someone if you're too swamped."

"I imagine I can take some time out of my busy schedule for an old friend."

He slapped back the rest of his beer and met her gaze again. He was going to be living in the same house as this newly sexualized Shannon, in the room next to hers. He might as well get this out so he could get on with things. "You're still a beauty," he said, his low voice carrying over a sad Irish love song. "More now than when you were in all those crazy pageants. You must have every man with a heartbeat after you, Princess. Every one."

The blush that blossomed on her cheeks spread like a light show. He used to make her blush as a parlor trick, something that would make her furious and hopefully storm off to her room. Now he found the contrast of her pale skin and the fire of her emotions far too fascinating.

"You're going to cause trouble, aren't you, Nate Brenner?" she asked, just loudly enough for him to hear.

"As much as humanly possible," he admitted. Then he smiled, because what the hell else was there to do about it? "Will you excuse me?"

"Sure," she said, her look suspicious.

Close to the bar he decided beer wasn't going to cut it. He ordered a boilermaker and drank it down right there on the spot.

"Is he?"

Shannon almost dropped her glass at the whisper behind her. It was Ariel, who didn't seem at all sorry for sneaking up on her like a thief. "Is who what?"

"Single." Ariel had to lift her head to see Nate standing with Danny in the midst of the crowd. Midnight, and hardly anyone had left the now stifling room.

"Yes, he is," Shannon said. "But he's not here for long."

"He doesn't have to be. All I'd need is one night."

Shannon frowned at her cousin. She'd been sweating—everyone was—and dark tendrils of hair were stuck to her face and neck. The way Ariel gasped for breath was more a result of the dancing she'd been up to than her interest in Nate… Still, Shannon could be mistaken about that. Ariel looked ready to pounce.

"If I do put him on a card, you'll have to be quick. It's first come, first served."

"Did you see how I caught the bouquet?" she asked. "I hate being single. I honestly do. It's a pity your guy isn't going to be around for the long haul. I like his laugh. That's huge for me. A sense of humor. You can get through most anything if you can find something to laugh about."

"You met him?"

Ariel sighed. "I did. He was great. But he was very involved in a conversation with Danny. Evidently I wasn't enough to distract him."

"Let me guess," Shannon said. "Notre Dame?"

Ariel rolled her eyes. "I swear, I could have stripped

right down to nothing and neither of them would have blinked."

"I doubt that. But I don't think they've seen each other since college. All those games to catch up on."

"At least he was funny."

"Humor's on the top of my list, too," Shannon said. "Along with shared values. And kindness."

"Don't forget great in the sack," Ariel said, still craning her neck to gaze at Nate.

"I can't help you with that one."

"You've never…?"

"No. Nothing remotely like that."

"Pity."

"Not really. He left when I was thirteen."

"God, it's broiling in here. Can't they open some windows?"

"I don't think it'll help. There's a hundred and fifty drunk people dancing like fools."

Ariel grinned at her. "It's wonderful, isn't it? I want my wedding to be just like this. Friendly, open. Plenty of booze and good food. If I ever have a wedding."

"That's what the trading cards are for." Shannon thought about how Rebecca Thorpe and Jake Donnelly were living together now. Part-time in Brooklyn and part-time in the Upper East Side. Shannon had the feeling they'd end up married. They were wildly in love.

"You, too, huh?"

Shannon must have let her envy show. "Yes, I would very much like to be married. So far my dates have been fun. But no magic."

Ariel shook her head. "Sometimes I wonder if magic is too much to hope for."

"Of course it's not," Shannon said. "A little bit of magic is in every good love story. I'm sure of it."

THE BROWNSTONE WAS A RELIC of a New York long gone. All three stories in the row house belonged to the Fitzgerald family, and since the third grade it had been more a home to Nate than his own.

At noon, the taxi pulled away, leaving him with his suitcase and duffel bag. The traditional wedding hangover lingered, but even so, approaching the red door on 3rd Avenue in Gramercy Park made him feel like a kid. The last time he'd been there had been pre-NYU. Before Danny went to study graphic design in Boston.

He banged on the knocker, the one Mr. Fitz had replaced after the Baseball Incident. Nate liked this one better. It was in the shape of a shillelagh, and it was loud.

Mrs. Fitz opened the door and, yeah, he was ten again, or fourteen, or eight, and all the years in between and around because she looked the same to him. Her hair was mostly gray now, but for a pale woman who seemingly had more freckles than skin, he saw remarkably few signs of the passing years. Then there was her frown. She wore it most of the time, and it put some people off. But he knew better. That was Danny's mom, worrying about her brood. She'd always said life in her house was most frightening when it got quiet, and she'd been right.

"Get a move on, Nathan—" and there was a hint of a brogue even though she'd been born and raised in New York "—you're letting in all the flies."

He dragged his rolled case and duffel bag across the threshold into the entry hall, then put the duffel on the big wooden bench, almost expecting his snow boots to be underneath on the boot mat. "It's good to be home," he said.

When he turned to smile at Mrs. Fitz, she was smiling right back, a rare and wonderful sight. "As long as we live here, boyo."

He wanted to throw his arms around her neck, it was so terrific to see her again. She'd been a major part of his life, and he didn't think of her often enough. But as big as their hearts were, the Fitzgeralds weren't huggers. Except for Shannon apparently.

"I imagine you'll be wanting lunch. You should eat first because Myles and Alice are still in his old room. Everyone slept in after the party, the drunken hooligans."

"Who you calling a hooligan?"

It was Danny, coming down the stairs, looking like a madman with his hair sticking out all over the place, unshaven, wearing some god-awful zombie T-shirt.

"Ah, I see why," Danny said. "We're in for it now."

"You two can set the dining room table." Mrs. Fitz headed toward her kitchen, but she made sure they heard. "My God, there's nine of us. You'll need to bring in chairs."

"So the whole crew stayed over?"

"To be fair," Danny said, scratching his belly as if he was alone in his bedroom, "Shannon and Brady live here. But Tim and me and the married ones, we had to stay. Nobody was taking a train at three in the morning."

Nate slipped off his coat and hung it on one of the wooden pegs that lined the entry hall. "Whatever happened to Gayle?"

Danny's brow furrowed. "Boston Gayle?"

Nate nodded.

"She kicked me out while I was in my boxers. Thought I'd slept with her best friend. Truth was, I had, but we didn't do anything but sleep. Completely innocent. Gayle didn't care, though." He started walking to the kitchen, now scratching his jean-covered butt. "She called me an evil bastard who had no class."

"Go figure." Nate trailed after his buddy, and everywhere his gaze rested he found another piece of his past. He'd fallen against the edge of the massive wooden dining room table, running when there'd been a very strict rule against it. In his defense, Myles had been chasing him, and Myles was six years older and mean.

Nate walked through the kitchen to the pantry door and swung it open. Ignoring the massive amounts of stores Mrs. Fitz kept on hand, enough to feed an army, instead he checked out the marks on the height chart etched on the wall. There was his name, alongside Tim and Myles and Brady and Danny. No Shannon, though. He hadn't remembered that. Still didn't know why.

"Please tell me there's coffee made."

Nate knew it was Shannon behind him, but her voice was as grown-up as the woman herself. Despite his complete and total awareness that she was no longer a child, his memories were in flux. He peeked out from the pantry to see her in her belted robe, her hair hanging over her right shoulder.

It shouldn't have been real, that color, but it was. They'd gone to Coney Island or out to the seashore, and no one ever got lost because all they had to do was look for that firecracker hair in the crowd.

Of course, she'd always gotten sunburned, even after Mrs. Fitz slathered her with goop. Nothing could protect that white skin, not umbrellas, not T-shirts, not the awful zinc on her nose.

"Oh." Her hand went to her hair, then just as quickly lowered. "You're here."

He came out of the pantry. "Just arrived. Currently on table-setting duty."

"My mother's a slave driver."

"I heard that, missy. You'd best get your coffee and get dressed. We have a houseful to feed."

Shannon turned to her mom standing by the stove. "There isn't one person in this house who isn't capable of fixing their own lunch. Not one." She had her hands on her hips, and Nate was taken aback again that she'd developed so many curves. It didn't seem possible. But then, he'd done some changing, too.

"You know your brothers. Left to their own devices, they'll eat nothing but garbage."

"Then that's what they deserve. Garbage." She turned back to Nate. "Don't bother asking who buys the candy and chips and cookies and cake and every horrible, calorie- and fat-laden food in New York."

"I wouldn't think of it."

"Then you learned something hanging around here all those years."

"That your mother is generous and wants her sons to be happy? Yeah, I got that one."

Mrs. Fitz nodded and kept on stirring what smelled like beef stew. Shannon smiled at him, patted his arm and went to the big coffee urn that took up half of the completely inadequate counter.

The house was huge, but that was mostly in height. Eight- and nine-foot ceilings, but small rooms. The old oak table where he'd eaten countless bowls of oatmeal dwarfed the breakfast nook. Even the living room barely fit the furniture. How many games he'd watched on those covered couches and chairs. He couldn't begin to guess. Didn't matter what season, if there was a game on anywhere on television, the Fitzgerald men were glued to it.

And there'd been snacks followed by huge dinners of meat and potatoes and enough cabbage to choke a horse. "That's what's missing," he said.

Danny, who was now pouring his coffee, Shannon, who was drinking hers, and Mrs. Fitz were all staring.

"Cabbage," he said, only then realizing he'd made a strategic error. He couldn't very well announce that he'd missed the stink. "I'm looking forward to some nice corned beef and cabbage soon, Mrs. Fitz. I still think about it all these years later."

"Well, you'll have it as you're staying more than a week," she answered, turning back to the heavy pot. "And since we had the new exhaust put in, it doesn't make the house smell to holy hell."

He grinned and shook his head. This was so much better than a hotel. He should have thought of asking to stay before he'd left Indonesia.

"Danny tells me you work with refugees," Mrs. Fitz said as she wiped her hands on a tea towel.

"Most of the time, yeah." Large white plates were put in his hands, and Danny led him to the table carrying a bunch of silverware. "I work for The International Rescue Committee. They set my agenda."

"Well, don't stop." Mrs. Fitz waved impatiently for him to continue. "Tell us what that means."

"I show up after a natural disaster and help plan and implement redevelopment. We try to recreate villages and towns as much as we can, even if a new design would be better. It's disorienting having everything you know ripped away in a tsunami or an earthquake. So we study old pictures, drawings and blueprints and figure out how to give people back their equilibrium first, then we add a few extras."

Shannon wasn't drinking even though her cup was at her mouth, and she wasn't even standing near her mom and yet he was watching her. He found Mrs. Fitz again. "It's challenging work, but very satisfying."

"I can't imagine."

She couldn't, Nate was sure of it. Not the conditions, not the sweat, the devastation, the utter anguish in every breath.

It was suddenly quiet, a rare thing in the Fitzgerald household, and he wished he hadn't gone into detail. No, it wasn't a pretty picture and better that people understood that not everyone enjoyed a comfortable middle-class life, but Shannon's empathetic expression both pleased him and made him want to kick himself.

Mrs. Fitz finally broke the silence. "Take Nate upstairs, Shannon. He hasn't seen the changes yet."

"Now?" Shannon said.

"You'd rather wait and let the food get cold?"

"Come on," she said to Nate. "I'll give you a tour." One hand had a death grip on her coffee mug, the other was in her robe pocket. "You're going to love what Mom did with Danny's room."

"Hey," Danny said. "He's supposed to be helping me set the table. And my room's a mess."

"You've only been here one night," Mrs. Fitz said. "What have you done?"

"Nothing, Ma. Nothing to worry about."

Nate had no problem leaving Danny to finish the job by himself, and even less of a problem following Shannon up the stairs. He wanted to check out the pictures that had dotted the old ivy wallpaper, but he ended up watching the sway of her hips instead.

3

She'd been one of those kids who loved the limelight, who glowed when she danced and sang and posed. Nate had been roped into attending far too many of her recitals and pageants. He'd been bored out of his gourd, but he'd gone. He and Danny had done their best to cause trouble, and they'd usually succeeded. So it hadn't been all for nothing. But she'd never swayed like that.

Shannon led him to Danny's old room, where Nate had spent the night hundreds of times. She grinned as she pushed the door open, and he peeked before stepping in.

"A sewing room?"

"Not just a sewing room," Shannon said, nudging him forward. "A library, a tea room, a knitting parlor and a quiet room. Mostly a place to escape from the heathens and their games."

"I didn't know your mother sewed. Or knit. Or read."

"She's...expanding her horizons," Shannon said, although there was more to it than that if he correctly read her raised brows.

"Has she retired?"

"Yep, she still does the books for the plant when

I'm swamped, but she decided when Brady took over as manager that she was going to spend time on things that weren't cooking or cleaning."

Speaking of, Danny's clothes were spread over a very comfortable-looking recliner, what probably was a daybed when it wasn't a mess of linens, and even over the doorknob of the closet. "At least one of your brothers hasn't changed."

Shannon leaned toward Nate and lowered her voice, her breath warm and sweet touching his skin. "He's actually doing really well at the advertising firm. Don't tell him I said so, but he's good. He's got a gift."

Too busy inhaling her scent, he almost missed his cue. "Okay, I must be in the wrong house. You? Saying nice things about Danny?"

"It's probably because I don't see him very often. Absence makes my tolerance stronger."

"I don't think that's how that saying's supposed to go."

"It's true, though," she said, eyeing the pile of yarn that had been pushed to the side. "Be warned. You won't leave here without at least a half-dozen new wool scarves."

"I'm working in Indonesia. The average yearly temperature is eighty degrees with ninety-percent humidity."

"As if that'll dissuade her. Oh, and they'll be hideous colors, too."

"I look forward to it."

"No, you don't," she said as she went back to the hallway. "But you can give them away. They are definitely warm."

"What about your room?"

"Mine? It's still too small."

"I'd like to see it," he said.

For a long stretch of barely breathing, Shannon stared at him, her lips parted. Then she moistened them, the tip of her tongue taking a nervous swipe. "Why?" she asked finally.

"Why?" Shit, he felt as if he were twelve again, caught trying to snatch a peek at Mr. Fitz's *Playboy*. "I'm curious about grown-up Shannon's natural habitat."

She shrugged. "Suit yourself. It's two doors down."

"I know." He shoved his hands in his pockets, wondering if crashing here was the right decision. It wasn't as if he couldn't afford to stay in a hotel. Which was probably more convenient. The real problem was Shannon. He hadn't expected her, not this version. "Is this going to be too weird?"

"What?" she asked, widening her eyes, but she didn't fool him for a minute. Her pupils were dilated and the pulse at the side of her neck beat as fast as his own.

"Maybe this isn't a good idea."

"Don't be silly." She laid a hand on his arm, then proved his point by withdrawing a moment too quickly. "We'll practically have the whole floor to ourselves. Brady's room is down the hall but he spends most nights at his girlfriend's place."

He had no business being so pleased about that last fact. No business at all.

FOR EVERYONE'S SAKE SHE HAD to snap out of this case of nerves and act naturally. So he wanted to see her bedroom. Not only was she making too much of it, but it also wasn't as if he hadn't seen it before. Usually with her screaming at him and Danny to get out and stay out, or yelling for her mom, or throwing something that was handy. But it wasn't a little girl's room anymore, and he wasn't that Nate.

He paused as they reached her door. "It occurs to me I should have asked about this first. As in giving you warning, and not just, hey, I want to see your room."

She smiled. "I'm not like the savages. My room is neat enough for surprise visits." She saw the uncertainty flicker in his eyes, and she shrugged. "I think it's going to take us all some time to adjust."

He turned. "You think we'll still like each other?"

"Still? I don't think we ever liked each other," Shannon said. "But then we were kids, and being my brother's best friend, it was your duty to torment me."

"And now?"

She looked into his warm, direct gaze and her body tightened. "Annoy me and I'll short-sheet your bed."

"Ah, so the room comes with maid service." Nate grinned, making him seem more like the boy she remembered and she relaxed a bit.

"Dream on." She moved to her closed door, her hand on the knob. "Go ask Mom about maid service. See what she says."

Nate winced and acted as if he'd been wounded. "You are trying to get rid of me. I don't know why your parents put up with me to begin with."

"Because they're big old softies. They don't even ask for me or Brady to pay rent, and when I started paying them anyway, I discovered they were putting my checks into a savings account for me."

"That's nice."

"My point exactly. With the benefit of hindsight, I believe they thought you needed the security of a big family."

He smiled, but it was more out of pathos than anything else. "My folks tried. They did. They loved us. They didn't have a gift for child rearing."

"Then isn't it good you had a backup plan?"

"Brilliant, even in third grade."

"Now I'm seeing the old Nate." She felt more like herself, as if they'd turned a corner. Not a huge one, but enough to start with. "So, ready for the reveal? God, it's hard to admit I still live here, even though it's becoming common again for people my age, no thanks to the recession."

"I like that you do. You've always been connected to your clan. I envy that."

"Depends on why I do it." She opened her door and stepped back to let him in.

He didn't go far, only a few steps, but she noticed he looked at everything. Her queen bed with the pastel sheets, the hint of lilac on the walls and in the reading chair. She wondered if he remembered the posters of all those boy bands, and Doogie Howser and Jonathan Taylor Thomas. Everything had been pink back then and had ruffles. There'd been a canopy, naturally, and stuffed animals. An entire display case of her tiaras and trophies from being Little Miss Gramercy Park and Little Miss Manhattan, and more than a dozen others. Some were still on display in the living room alongside the boys' sports awards.

"I was right," Nate said.

"About?"

"Your good taste. Although the room's not quite the same without that framed picture of Leonardo DiCaprio."

"Who was all of fourteen at the time."

He went to one of the pictures on the wall. It wasn't anything fancy. She'd found it at a local art festival, and she'd spent more on the frame than the picture. It was an ordinary bedroom, small and neat, and filled with light. There was an open book on the bedside table, a shawl left draped on a big chair. It was cozy and quiet, not something she'd felt often growing up.

"I don't spend a lot of time in houses anymore," he said. "Or beds. I'm lucky to get a cot sometimes. I've even gotten used to hammocks."

"What drew you away, Nate? Danny said you'd wanted to help after the tsunami, but he never said why."

Nate turned, and he looked so good, so content. He was wearing jeans, a Henley shirt, boots. She could picture him doing errands, getting his hands dirty. But once he'd grown out of his terrible years, before he'd gone away, she remembered him as a reader. He'd liked architecture and didn't seem unhappy that he was expected to follow in his father's footsteps. She'd been surprised at his humanitarian streak.

That sounded kind of awful when she thought about it so bluntly, but she'd never seen him go out of his way much. Admittedly, her perspective had been limited.

"I'm not sure. I don't think I was running to as much as I was running from."

"Was it so bad?"

"No. It's not as if I was abused or mistreated or anything like that. I don't know. I guess I had read too many books about adventures. I wanted some of my own before I settled down."

"From the looks of it you're not done yet."

"Nope. Not yet."

"How will you know?" she asked.

"When, you mean?"

Shannon nodded.

"No idea. I don't think too far into the future, to tell you the truth. Everything is so immediate and real in a way I have a hard time describing. It's interesting to be back here, to shift my perspective." He touched the edge of her bed. "I like your room. It's calm, and it's pretty, but there's still you all over it."

She would have liked to have asked him more about his other life, but she went with the program. "What do you mean, me all over it?"

He walked over to her dresser. "Playbills, perfume, ticket stubs, lectures. I'm surprised you didn't end up on the stage. You loved it so much as a kid."

"Some people would say I've made my life a stage."

"What would you say?"

She waved the comment away with her free hand. "Sales, marketing. It's all just acting, isn't it? Anyway, I imagine Mom is getting antsy. We should go down."

He nodded, but turned to take another sweeping look at her small room. "It's home but it isn't," Nate said softly.

Shannon wasn't sure if he was speaking to her or himself. "What?"

"I'm glad I'm here. I'd forgotten I had memories I wanted to keep."

"About New York?"

"No. This house. This family. You."

"Me? I was the pain-in-the-ass Princess. What would you want to remember about that?"

"You were the prettiest little girl I'd ever known. By the time I was getting ready for NYU, you'd gotten even more beautiful. Now, you're…"

She could feel the blush again and realized it was going to be a problem. "I'm…?"

He inhaled deeply. "We should go eat." He walked past her and out the door.

Shannon touched her cheeks, willing them to cool off, wondering what had just happened.

NATE HAD WOKEN UP BEFORE the alarm. He'd adjusted to the time change, being in the Northern Hemisphere, and the sounds of the city. He hadn't done as well with adjusting to the beds.

At the hotel he'd never found the sweet spot, so those nights had been crappy. Myles's bed was even worse. It sagged in the middle, so no matter where he started, he ended up sinking, his back curving unnaturally. While in the hottest shower he could stand, he'd debated changing rooms after Danny left, but that would be weird seeing as it was now Mrs. Fitz's sanctuary.

So, he'd work in a couple of massages while he was here. The shower had helped get the kinks out, but now he was running late. He finished shaving, then wiped the shaving cream away. Making sure the towel around his waist was secure, he opened the bathroom door and bumped right into Shannon.

He decided to ignore that his startled squeak was almost the same pitch as Shannon's. "Sorry, sorry."

She'd backed up a couple of steps, pulling the top of her robe together. "No, I just didn't expect…"

Her gaze had gone from his face to his chest. And stayed there. He checked. The towel hadn't fallen.

She let go of her robe to gesture at his body, at least from the neck down. "When did all that happen?"

He chuckled. He'd been a skinny kid, but he'd done a great deal of hard manual labor overseas, and when there were lulls, he kept himself ready. He returned her gesture, although his wave was focused more around the breast area. "When did all that happen?"

"Point taken," she said, with an uneasy laugh. "But hey. Nice."

"You, too."

"Now go away. I need to shower." She sounded friendly, unaffected, but he'd seen the telling blush as she pushed past him in a sudden hurry. "You better not have used up the hot water."

"Would I do that to you?"

She turned, her gaze flickering to his chest before meeting his eyes. "Please."

"Yeah, okay. But it wasn't my fault. Have you ever slept in Myles's bed? I kept waking up thinking I was being smothered."

"So, no hot water left?"

"I wouldn't linger if I were you." He couldn't, either. Not without embarrassing himself. Partly her fault, the way she'd looked at him.

Shannon sighed.

He accidentally brushed her arm. "I'm sorry. I'll be more considerate. I will. I haven't had to be for a while."

She stared at the place he'd touched her, and when she looked up again, he knew he was in trouble. She was a very beautiful woman. Not a kid, not a teen. And he'd spent a few hours of sleeplessness thinking about how pale her skin was and if all her hair was as stunningly red. He'd felt weird about that last night, but not now. He wanted her, and he was pretty damn sure she wanted him right back.

She cleared her throat, then hurried into the bathroom and shut the door.

It was a problem. He had no idea what the ground rules were. Except that he had no business being half-hard standing in the hallway. He made it to Myles's room in case Brady hadn't gone to his girlfriend's place last night, but Nate was acutely aware that the next door over was Shannon's bedroom. That she was taking a shower right this minute. Naked. Pale. Her nipples would be pink. Like the color of her blush.

Shit.

"WAIT," SHANNON SAID, pointing at Nate. "Come over here and stand in front of the fireplace."

"Why?" He glanced at his watch.

"It'll only take a second. I need a couple of pictures."

He frowned at her, but he was moving in the right direction. "For what?"

"Neighborhood blog. No big deal, but I edit the damn thing and I need filler."

"Wait a minute. What are you going to say?" He had reached the brick fireplace and placed his hand on the mantel.

She doubted he even realized he was posing, but she brought up her cell phone quickly, clicking as often as she could between flash charges. "You live a very adventurous and heroic life," she said, moving a bit to her right to get another angle. Then she zoomed in even closer. He looked great in his dark suit, no tie, off-white shirt with the top button undone. She wished she could have gotten him in his towel this morning, but then again, she probably wouldn't have been able to keep her hands steady.

She clicked again. "You're a native son. It'll make a great story."

"How many people read this blog of yours?"

"Oh, a lot."

"I'm not sure about this. There are people I don't want to see. I was hoping to keep the visit quiet."

"Oh, well, that's easy to solve. I'll run it after you're gone. And I'll make sure to say great things about your organization. I looked it up. You guys do fantastic work."

"Yeah, we do. And they'll appreciate the mention," he said, then glanced at his watch again. "I've got to go."

"Fine," she said, stealing one last picture.

"But I get to read it, and if I don't like it, you're not going to run it."

She wanted to argue, but it didn't really matter. She could easily skip writing a piece for the blog. This session was about the trading cards. "Deal," she said.

"Okay. See you tonight."

"Maybe Molly's?"

He smiled as he passed her. "Yeah, Molly's sounds great."

She watched him as he walked, still stunned at her reaction to his...to him. The thing was, she hadn't expected the change. He'd been one of those narrow boys, no ass, no chest to speak of. Like most of her brothers. Myles hadn't been that way, though, at least not after puberty hit. He'd gathered a harem when he got on the junior varsity football team, and that hadn't all been due to padding.

But Nate, he'd had an average, if slim, silhouette the last time they'd been to the community swimming pool. He'd been seventeen, she'd been twelve, and she'd threatened to drown him if he continued to splash her with his stupid cannonballs.

He wasn't average anymore. Not a muscle man, either, just, well, sculpted. Defined. Enough chest hair to be enticing instead of daunting, and those guns…who would have guessed?

She'd reacted. As any woman would. But being attracted to Nate seemed every kind of wrong.

She'd make his trading card first thing. Get him out on the market. It probably was good that she hadn't taken a picture of his naked chest. There'd be a riot at St. Marks.

Her mother's call from the kitchen snagged her attention, but a quick look at the clock got her moving. She had a huge day ahead, and now she was going to have to put together Nate's card.

It was possible that would have to wait. The lunch group wouldn't get together for another week. For now, she'd look at the pictures, make sure she had a winner. She hoped so. It would be difficult to come up with another excuse.

"I'll have something at the plant," Shannon said as she got her coat from the peg. "I'll be in and out all day."

"Don't get doughnuts," her mother said, popping up in the dining room. "Your father can't say no."

Shannon opened her mouth to object, then sighed. "How do you do that?"

"I'm your mother. You can't keep secrets from me."

"That's what you think," she said, putting her phone into her purse.

"You and Steven Patterson. Coney Island."

Shannon froze. "What are you talking about?"

Her mother laughed. "Don't try to fool me, missy."

It was time for Shannon to leave before she started thinking about that tattoo and her face gave her mother more ammunition. She opened the door, but only made it halfway out.

"At least the tattoo wasn't a tramp stamp," her mom called out. "That would have been really embarrassing."

Shannon closed the door behind her and blushed all five blocks to the subway.

NATE STOOD BEHIND THE barricade that separated the street from the construction zone. He had no idea how long he'd been standing, but when he sipped his coffee, it was lukewarm, leaning toward cold. The sign on the chain-link fence was as familiar to him as the sound of the cranes and earthmovers. Brenner & Gill. Even after he'd inherited half of the firm, the Brenner referred to his father, not himself. And in about fifteen minutes, he would be meeting with Albert Gill, his father's partner.

Nate had known Albert most of his life. Yet he didn't know Gill well. The basics, yes. His wife was Patty and he had two daughters, Melody and Harper. There had been Christmas dinners, because the Gills celebrated, and a couple of times they'd had Hanukkah dinners instead, even though Nate's family were barely observant. But the families had never been friends. His father hadn't had a gift for friendship, either. It was something of a miracle that he'd gotten married at all, given he preferred to be alone.

That's how they'd found him. Slumped over his drafting table on a Monday morning. He'd died the Friday before sometime between seven and midnight. According to the coroner's office, he'd gone quickly, hadn't felt a thing.

Nate had come back for the funeral, but he hadn't stuck around. It was a quiet business, and he'd been surprised to find that his mother and Leah had sat shivah for the whole week. Nate had worn a yarmulke, although he'd left it in the box by the door when he'd gone back to his hotel. His mother had made sure his old bedroom was left open for him, but he'd felt no need to stay.

And while he'd mourned his father, it wasn't what he'd been led to believe was normal. Frank Brenner had been more of an idea than a dad. He showed up at the important events, paid for most of Nate's college education, but their relationship had been about expectations and conditions. Since Nate had stopped even trying to be his father's ideal son after graduation, there'd been very little left.

Now he would meet with Albert over lunch, and they'd have an awkward half hour when they tried to reminisce. Nate hoped their meal would be delivered quickly. Food would be an essential distraction until they got to the heart of the matter.

Albert wanted out. It was the details Nate didn't know, the considerations. He wanted to read Albert as he spoke, figure out what he could before Nate met with his attorney.

There was a lot of money at stake. Building commercial crap paid well. The firm had a great reputation. But it wasn't going to be close to a handshake deal. Albert had run the business. He'd made the deals, set the terms, got the financing. Nate's father had designed the buildings, coordinated the construction plans. Albert had many, many friends. He was good with people and he was smart. No doubt he wanted a sizable amount.

What he'd get was his fair share. Nate headed to the restaurant, four blocks from the construction site, prepared to be read in return. He was up for it. He wasn't afraid of much these days. Too much time spent facing reality.

He had to admit, though, he was looking forward to the game. He'd always liked chess.

4

Despite the horrible day, as Shannon reached the entrance to Molly's Pub, her pulse and breathing quickened. Nate was there already. He'd texted her ten minutes ago, which was a good thing, as she'd been so caught up in looking at the receivables she'd lost track of time.

He'd said not to worry, he was relaxing with a pint. She glanced at the window that announced with green lettering that this was Molly's Shebeen before she opened the heavy wooden door.

It took a moment for her eyes to adjust, and there was Nate, sitting three booths from the wood-burning fireplace that was fed and stoked all winter. She hung up her coat, then went toward him, her excitement mounting.

It would be fun to talk to him, was all. She wasn't even thinking about how he'd looked in that towel this morning. Okay, she was thinking a little about that, but she wasn't dwelling. That would be wrong. Foolish. The minute she started truly contemplating Nate as more than a friend, things got uncomfortable. He was family, and while it wasn't technically inappropriate, it was close enough to make her squirm.

His grin, however, made her light up. "Finally. I'm starving to death."

"Why didn't you order something, then?" she asked as she slid into the seat across from him.

"Because I'm polite."

"Don't be ridiculous. You're only polite when you want something. Is Danny coming?"

"Nope." Nate took a swallow from his half-empty Guinness. "It's just you and me."

She picked up the menu although she didn't need to look at it. Molly's was literally just down the street from her house, and she'd been coming here long before she'd been legal. Not that they'd let her sit with the customers. She'd been escorted to the back room, where she'd been fed and given cold milk with her dinner, and no matter how she'd explained that in Ireland even kids got to drink beer, she was denied the pleasure until she'd hit her twenty-first birthday. Or so she'd have her family believe.

"How was your day?" she asked, content to listen to Nate all evening.

"Interesting." He pulled out the *New York Times* classified section where he'd circled a bunch of listings. "It's never not going to be insanely expensive to live in this city."

"You're right," she said as she noticed Ellen coming over with two beers on a tray.

"How are you, Shannon?"

"Good, thanks."

Ellen put a perfectly chilled and poured Guinness in front of her, then gave Nate another. "You two want food?"

"God, yes," Nate said. "Cheeseburger with blue for me."

Shannon started to order her regular spinach salad, but said, "The same for me, please," instead.

Nate's brow rose first, then Ellen's.

"I've had a bad day. I'm hungry. So you can both be quiet."

Ellen left, and Nate leaned forward, elbows on the table. "What happened?"

"Don't want to talk about it. Tell me what you've found in the paper."

"Ah," he said, frowning at the real-estate section. "Everyone told me this is the best time to buy, because everything's going for rock-bottom prices. Rock bottom of what? I can't find a decent two-bedroom town house with an on-site manager for less than a million and a half."

"It's still Manhattan," she said. "People keep coming, and they keep paying."

"Crazy is what it is." He looked up at her with wide eyes, and even in the dim amber light, she could feel his interest. In the conversation, of course. "Your house has got to be worth many millions. You could sell that sucker and retire tomorrow, all of you. Move somewhere, pretty much anywhere but London or Paris, and live like kings for the rest of your life. And if you sold the plant, too?"

"Yeah, well, that's not going to happen. The house has been with us for generations. We're not about to let it go. Not the plant, either, dammit."

His open mouth closed and his excited gaze turned to concern. "I didn't mean anything by that," he said. "I wasn't serious."

She drank some so she could get her equilibrium

back. After she patted the foam off her upper lip, she smiled at him. "I know. I shouldn't have snapped at you. As I said, bad day."

"Did you eat lunch?"

Shannon blinked at him. "Uh, yeah. Why?"

"You used to get cr—out of sorts when you waited too long to eat. When we were kids."

"I admit, I did get cranky years ago, and all right, yes, I probably should have eaten more today. How did you even remember that?"

"Funny, huh, what sticks?" He tapped his temple. "Let's just say I have a lot of blackmail material stored away up here."

She feigned covering her mouth for a cough that didn't do much to hide her saying, "Underoos."

"Ouch," he said. "Although, I seem to recall a My Little Pony phase that went on for an incredibly long time."

"Those were adorable. And very appropriate for a child my age."

"I wasn't wearing Underoos to high school, you know."

"No, I didn't," Ellen said, and Shannon and Nate looked over at the grinning waitress. She put their silverware down and patted Nate on the head. "It's good to have you back for a visit," she said, then wandered off.

"I never realized how much the sawdust dampens sound," Nate said.

"I imagine everyone in the bar will be talking about your underwear in the next couple of days."

"And people wonder why I stay overseas."

Shannon reached for a napkin. She did wonder why he'd stayed away. And why he was so keen on selling

Brenner & Gill. But she didn't want serious tonight. She wanted to relax with her…friend.

NATE WANTED TO PUT HIS ARM around Shannon as they walked back to the house. It was close to midnight, stupidly cold, and he was so drawn to her it was a bad joke. Instead, he kept his hands in his pockets and tried to stop watching her long enough to prevent walking straight into a streetlight pole.

"I shouldn't have had that last beer," Shannon said.

"No, you probably shouldn't have."

She slowed her step and bumped his shoulder with hers. "You had more to drink than I did."

"We weren't talking about me. I should have stopped after my second Guinness. But come on. Guinness. At Molly's Shebeen. How am I supposed to resist that, hmm?"

"You're right," she said. "You were perfectly justi-fied. I, on the other hand, was reckless and foolish. I should be ashamed."

"Well, hell. If you're going to waste shame on some-thing like having an extra beer, you should give up right now."

Her laughter warmed him like a hot toddy. "What, you want me to rob a bank? Steal a car? Have an illicit affair?"

"Those are all legitimately shame-worthy, yes. Al-though I never said that shame had to come along with a prison sentence. You still need to have good judgment. So that leaves illicit affairs."

"I don't have anyone to be illicit with."

"No?"

She grabbed his arm and pulled him close. There wasn't enough beer in Molly's to slow down his heart.

"You almost walked into that pole," she said as she released him.

"Damn, I thought—"

"What?" she asked, and he shook his head. "You thought what?"

"Nope."

She studied him for a second. "Coward."

"Yep."

She laughed. "I could get it out of you if I wanted."

"Hey, go for it. I welcome the challenge." Suppressing a smile, he kept walking. She hated a dare, and he doubted that had changed.

"You have some nerve bringing up good judgment," she muttered. "I'd like to know where you got your measuring stick."

He had a totally juvenile remark at the tip of his tongue, which only proved how deeply irresponsible he'd been about the beer. Though the pole—that had nothing to do with drinking and everything to do with the illicit-affair remark. "Experience has taught me not to sweat the small stuff."

This time Shannon stopped completely. "You must be drunk if you're throwing that old clunker at me. How do you know what the small stuff is? One extra drink could be devastating."

"But you're not driving or operating heavy machinery. You're walking a block to your home, and you're safely accompanied by a man who knows how to kick the crap out of anyone who might try anything untoward. Therefore, you having a third beer isn't a big deal."

"What do you mean you know how to kick the crap out of anyone?"

"I have skills."

He couldn't see her smile in the shadow between streetlights, but he would swear on his life he could feel it.

"Would those be mad skills?" she asked in the most smart-ass, taunting voice he could imagine.

"They would," he said, realizing that with every word he was digging himself a deeper hole.

"Of the martial-arts variety?"

"And if I said yes?"

She poked him in the chest with her index finger. "You still have every single comic you ever bought, don't you?" Poke. "You store them in airtight containers and don't let other humans touch them." Poke. "You don't have to rent your costume for Halloween. Ever."

He grabbed her poking hand and walked her toward a streetlight until he was sure they could see each other well. "I do have a hell of a comic collection, which is worth a great deal, by the way. I do store some of them in a temperature- and humidity-controlled storage facility because of their value. I do not have costumes in my wardrobe, however. But I've been known to go to comic conventions and I keep up with the industry. I like comics. I like graphic novels. And someday, if you agree not be bitchy about it, I would like to show you why."

There was a moment of silence. Not just from Shannon, but from the street, from the city. A fleeting lull in the traffic, the subway vibrations, the chatter of pedestrians. He heard her inhale, sharp and startled, as if the last thing in the world she'd expected was his little speech.

He was surprised himself, so that seemed fair. He'd had no preparation, though, for how she was looking at him. As if he was someone unexpected. Someone interesting in a way he shouldn't be.

Good. That's what he'd wanted. And if he hadn't had the extra beer, he'd lean over right this second and kiss her until she cried uncle. But he was tipsy enough to know that he was treading on thin ice, illustrated perfectly by his use of the word *tipsy*.

Both of them having inappropriate thoughts didn't mean the thoughts were no longer inappropriate. He had one place he considered home in this world, and to risk that, he'd have to be sober as a judge and twice as sure.

"I'd like that," she said, her voice a breathless whisper in the quiet. "A lot."

"Yeah?"

Her nod was slow but it still made that gorgeous hair of hers move forward on her shoulder. He raised his hand, but the last vestiges of good sense stopped him from carrying out the gesture. He was going to be at the Fitzgeralds' for several weeks. There would be time to figure things out. Time to see where the lines were drawn.

The last thing on earth he wanted was to be ashamed about anything to do with Shannon. So tonight, he'd walk her home and he'd sleep it off.

Tomorrow he might curse himself for letting this chance go by, but better safe than sorry when there was so much at stake.

Dammit, he was going to wake up to his second hangover in two days. The sooner he got back to his real life the better off he'd be. He looked again at Shannon as they reached the steps of the brownstone. Then again, as long as he had to be here, he might as well enjoy the visit.

SHANNON HADN'T SEEN NATE at breakfast, and she was almost late because she'd dawdled, hoping. Then she'd castigated herself the whole way to the plant. Last night hadn't been a date. She wasn't sure precisely what it had been, but not a date.

Despite the extra beer, she'd stayed up far too late. Her brain wouldn't stop. Thoughts of his voice, his scent, how he looked in a suit were only the beginning. She imagined vividly his friendly touch on the small of her back sliding past her waist until his palm slowly brushed over the curve of her behind.

A smile, then as his gaze hit her lips, the heat of his breath, the brush of a tentative kiss.

An innocent look turned smoldering, unmistakable want.

By the time she'd entered her office, she knew her first order of business wasn't going to be a call to the deputy commissioner in charge of Union Square Park. That and everything else on her list would wait while she turned her total attention to creating Nate's trading card. Maybe then she could stop obsessing.

He was going to be staying at the house for several weeks at least, and wouldn't it be nice and smart to hook him up with one of her friends from the lunch exchange? He'd be otherwise occupied while she pulled a new card or two for herself. The next lunch exchange meeting was coming up soon, and she had six new trading cards to prepare including Nate's.

She decided to do the copy first. After locking her office door, she opened a blank trading card template and started by typing.

His profession was easy: architect and urban planner. No need to talk about his humanitarian efforts on the card. That information would be much more dramatic coming out when she talked him up.

Marry, Date or One-Night Stand, another simple answer: Date. Only, wait. She deleted that and entered One-Night Stand. Then she deleted that. He certainly wasn't Marry. Come on, she'd know if he wanted to get married. He wouldn't be rushing back to Bali as quickly as he could if that were the case. Or would he?

He hadn't said anything about a woman. Did that mean there wasn't one? Or was she someone exotic and adventurous, a woman who would steer clear of anything to do with New York. Who lived on the edge. Maybe a doctor from the World Health Organization, someone who put herself at risk to save lives in regions fraught with danger.

That made sense. Nate had changed so much, and wasn't there always a woman behind that kind of transformation? She should have known there was more to it. He'd probably gone to Indonesia full of the best intentions. But then he'd met her, probably saving a small village cut off from civilization, and he'd helped her, both of them hot and sweaty, sleeping in bits and snatches as they slowly patched together the survivors. They were bound to be hyperaware of each other, especially when he heard her accent. French, had to be French. She'd be beautiful, naturally.

Shannon sighed as she realized she'd typed a long line of *B*s all the way across her document.

Okay, she would go with One Night Stand and move on.

His Favorite Restaurant was easy. It was undoubtedly something in Paris or Hong Kong or Monaco but screw that, she was going with Molly's Pub. He was certainly comfortable there. He'd laughed a lot. He'd made her laugh. His stories were preposterous and creative. She could thank his comic books for that, she was sure.

That tale he'd told last night about pirates? Seriously, pirates? Yes, she'd read about Somali pirates in the paper, and yes, the frequency and brutality of their attacks on ships had made the waters of the Indian Ocean extremely dangerous, but Nate Brenner, fighting off armed bandits with a cricket bat and a tin gas can? He'd painted quite a picture, even though she knew the pirates he'd been talking about had nothing in common with broadswords and buried treasure.

She scratched out Molly's Pub. That wouldn't work. She went there too much herself, and the prospect of having to watch him with a date made her stomach feel a little off. Which was stupid. She'd be the one setting him up with the date so she'd know the woman, and wasn't that the whole point of the trading cards? Making sure the matches were suitable and safe?

Oh, hell, she'd have to come back to favorite restaurant.

Anyway, next was his Secret Passion. Shannon exhaled loudly, thought about putting down comic books, but she didn't type the words. Instead, she went to the break room, nodding at the people on the floor. They were doing two very large textbook runs for a university press, which was good, and all but one of the other presses were busy with baseball trading cards. It looked as though the company was standing on a solid foundation. Only she knew the depth of the corrosion of customers slipping away, and how precarious their situation was for the long haul.

No, that wasn't quite true. Every walk through the plant was full of evidence to the contrary. The long looks, the fear in their employees' eyes. They knew.

They were on the front lines, after all. Especially painful was the change in her relationships with two of her press operators, Daphne and Melissa. The three of them had been close. Now they avoided her gaze and talked about her behind her back.

It was Shannon's parents who didn't quite get the dire picture. The two of them weren't involved in the nitty-gritty of the plant any longer, and she was glad of it. If things went Shannon's way, they would never know. Because she would fix it. She had a battle plan. At least some of the new customers she'd been working on were bound to come through.

She couldn't think about it now. She got her coffee, put on a smile and returned to her office. She would finish the cards and scan the photos. Tonight, after hours, she'd do the typesetting and the printing. She'd complete the job early tomorrow, and that would be that. She'd be ready for the lunch exchange, she'd stop thinking of Nate as anything other than family and she'd get on with her job.

Someone had to save Fitzgerald & Sons.

After stopping to answer yet another surly question from Melissa, Shannon entered her office not feeling any better from the break.

She woke up her computer monitor, trading the screen saver for Nate's card, and almost dropped her coffee. Her heart slammed in her chest at the picture on the screen.

It was a photograph of an obviously abandoned printing plant. No caption, but then none was needed.

A wave of anxiety swept through her, forcing her to turn away from the computer. A press of the intercom brought a quick response from Brady. "What's up?"

"Can you come to my office, please?" Her voice had wobbled, dammit.

"Shannon? What's wrong?"

"Just come, Brady. Now." She disconnected the intercom and took several deep breaths. She wanted to get rid of the image, but her brother needed to see it. This wasn't the first incident of what—vandalism? protest?—although it was the most brazen. She'd been in the break room for all of five minutes. Enough time to pour, to stir in milk and a sugar substitute. Her conversation with Melissa had been uncomfortable, but brief. Whoever had done this had raced.

Brady had raced, too, because he was at her door amazingly quickly. "What happened?"

She nodded toward the computer.

His sigh held so much of her own frustration. "What do they think this will accomplish?"

She turned to her older brother. He was a redhead, but not like her. His hair was dark and so were his eyebrows. He was also a hell of a decent guy. Of all the brothers, he was the most down-to-earth. He liked running the plant, knew the machines as if they were his own creations. Nothing was too complex for Brady except the human capacity to be cruel.

"They're scared. They feel impotent and terrified."

He gesticulated wildly even before speaking, which only happened when he was extremely riled up. "They think this will help save the shop? Save their jobs?"

"That's just it. They don't know what to do."

"But you've told them the truth. You've been there to help them when they needed it. Just last week you gave Terrance an advance on his wages. Again. At this rate, he'll never pay us back."

"It's for medical bills. Taking away the health plan

was a horrible blow." She inhaled deeply. Brady wasn't totally on the mark. It wasn't so much that she'd told the whole truth as she hadn't lied.

"Would they rather we closed down? Would that be better?"

She shook her head. There weren't words. She was doing everything in her power, but it wasn't enough. Never enough.

All she could do was keep trying. So she sat, and she got rid of the picture on her screen, found where it had been loaded on her desktop and deleted it. She'd have to lock her door now, whenever she left, even to go to the bathroom.

This wasn't how it was supposed to be. This was a good company. A conscientious company. She wished she could understand how things had spun so far out of control.

She saved Nate's trading card in her private folder and clicked out of that program. There was no time for frivolous matters. She had to get new customers before it all went to hell.

5

"YOU'RE UP EARLY."

Nate jumped at Shannon's voice, although he covered it quickly with a cough. It was 6:30 a.m. and it wasn't as if he hadn't expected someone to be in the kitchen—the light was on, coffee made—but he hadn't seen her sitting at the table in the breakfast nook. For reasons that only made sense when they'd been nine, he and Danny used to sit underneath that table for breakfast every morning until they did something horrible and messy and had to report to the big table in the dining room, where the first and last meals of the day had been family affairs, complete with table settings and lessons in manners.

It was yet another adjustment to find Shannon in the nook, half in shadow, in the now familiar pink robe. "I'm house hunting," he said, bringing down a large mug from the cupboard.

He'd missed her the past few days. According to Mr. Fitz, she'd been staying late at work, and Nate and Danny had been catching up with friends at old haunts. He'd looked for Shannon, though, each morning. Each night. Hoping he hadn't spooked her on their walk home from Molly's. He didn't think so, he'd shown restraint, but seeing her smile now he knew for certain things were okay between them. And up to him to keep it that way.

"Where are you looking?" Sleep still clung to her voice, lowering the pitch and giving her a sexy rasp he had no business thinking about.

Great. His resolve had lasted all of two seconds. "Starting in the East Village. Then Greenwich and SoHo if there's time."

"All town houses?"

"The Realtor convinced me not to be so set on a specific type of building. She's basing her suggestions on the maintenance companies."

"That makes sense," Shannon said, "considering you won't be around if something bad happens."

The scent of the coffee was enough to kick him into the next phase of waking up. He hadn't showered, hadn't done anything but put on his robe. It was damn cold to be barefoot, but he hadn't brought slippers and hadn't thought to put on socks. The chill hurried him to the bench across from Shannon's. "You should come with me."

She coughed, having just sipped some of her own coffee. "Just come with you, huh? Blow off my whole day?"

"I'll buy you a good lunch. And you can say rude things about people's decorating choices."

"Why would I want to do that?"

He gave her a look that told her she wasn't dealing with an amateur. "You couldn't have changed that much."

"It's not rude if it's constructive criticism."

"Like hell."

She smiled at him behind her Gramercy Park mug. Her skin stopped him, his own cup an inch off the table. She looked as if she were made of cream and silk. Something that couldn't possibly exist in nature. Like the ads in the magazines that made every flaw disappear with the magic of airbrushing. But he was close, and she was as real as anything. He ached to touch her, not just on her cheek, although that's where he'd start. He could barely imagine the feel of her inner thigh, what it would be like to rest his cheek on her tummy, right below her belly button.

"Okay, that's pretty creepy," Shannon said.

He put his cup down. "What?" He knew he'd been staring. So why was he playing dumb?

"You do that a lot," she said. "There's a pattern. Am I that different from who you remember?"

"Yes," he said, and he should have hesitated there. For a few seconds at least.

"Okay."

She sipped more coffee and, ahh, there it was. The blush. He wanted to watch it evolve in all its heated glory, but he'd already crossed the polite behavioral line.

What he didn't understand was the reason for the blush. Yes, he'd stared too long, and that was rude, but was she blushing because she was embarrassed at the attention? If he'd been anyone else, would she have blushed or would she have walked away from the situation? Was she reacting to the stare itself, or had she sussed that he was thinking about her sexually?

"Did you and Danny go out and cause havoc last night?"

A change in the subject was probably a good thing,

and he'd roll with it. "Well, I wouldn't go so far as to say havoc."

"Let me be the judge," she said. "But first, I need another coffee. You want a refill while I'm up?"

"I've barely touched mine, thanks."

He didn't hesitate to watch her cross the short distance to the giant coffee urn. The timer switch had to have been set at some ungodly hour for it to finish perking so early. So like Mrs. Fitz.

The thought of her mother vanished as his gaze ran down the back of Shannon in her belted robe. The curves killed him. She'd been so straight for so long. Now, he couldn't stop thinking of his hands on her waist. Shit, the desire to have her naked had become more and more acute with every passing night. He was the one blushing now, and he never did. He got too much enjoyment from crossing social boundaries. Blushing was for people who cared if they were offensive.

But wanting Shannon…he hadn't been able to talk his way around that issue. This new mind-set should've been squashed each time he went upstairs and was regaled with pictures of little Princess Shannon, the Shannon he'd known best. In her tiaras and her tutus, she was the essence of innocence. Not like those kids they put on parade today. She hadn't been made to look like a miniature centerfold. In fact, she hadn't been sexualized at all, thank God. She looked like a fairy, like a Disney character come to life.

Except she wasn't that child any longer. She was twenty-seven and she was single and only one thin wall separated their bedrooms at night.

He turned his head, stared hard at the refrigerator, which frankly wasn't that interesting, but he didn't want her to see his face at the moment. He wasn't a very good actor, and his want felt bigger than his ability to pretend.

If for no other reason than out of respect for Mr. and Mrs. Fitz, Shannon should be out-of-bounds. Maybe he needed to go back to staying at the hotel. He could make up some lie that wouldn't hurt any feelings. Anything would be easier than being so close when he had to keep his distance.

THE TOTE BAG FULL OF FROZEN Irish stew servings banged against Shannon's thigh as she walked down the path to the St. Marks basement door. For the first time since she'd joined the lunch exchange, Shannon wasn't looking forward to the gathering. She had new cards ready, as always in a box so she could pour them out in a cascade of eligible men; all the drama she could fit into a dreary kitchen basement. She'd go through the motions—it was expected, after all—but her heart wouldn't be in it.

Work had been eating Shannon alive. Aside from the Easter preparations, the baseball team shirts, posters and calendars and the regular day-to-day pressings and bindings, she hadn't gone a day without making cold calls, without visiting at least one new potential client, without placing at least a dozen business cards in likely and unlikely venues.

In between, every spare second, she'd been consumed with thoughts of Nate, then feel guilty, talk herself out of that, then start the cycle over again. Midnight after midnight found her wide-awake, coming up with new approaches to get clients, or, more frequently, remembering every detail of Nate in a towel, Nate at the bar, Nate in the hallway, Nate, Nate, Nate.

She was doing all she could to increase business at the plant, and today she'd make a stand in her madness over Nate. While she couldn't ask him to leave the house, she could send him on a date. Hopefully more than one. And, despite her insane schedule, she would go out on dates of her own. Every night, if necessary.

The thought of which made her feel sick.

It was the stress. So much of it, and so few opportunities to vent. Brady had enough of his own troubles, so she couldn't whine to him, and she didn't want to tell the other brothers because they couldn't be trusted not to blurt out something in front of her parents. Thank goodness for all those years of practicing to smile and acting cheerful at pageants.

As she opened the basement door she put one of those smiles in place, ratcheted up her enthusiasm and went inside. The sound of her friends helped make both smile and attitude more true, and by the time she was in the kitchen, she felt better.

Everyone stopped. It had been one of her favorite parts of the trading cards. The expectant hush, the anticipation, the possibilities. Her, center stage. It was Christmas every couple of weeks. No, she hadn't found her perfect man yet, but there were so many success stories. She'd done that. Not alone, but the idea had been hers, and why couldn't she find something equally wonderful that would bring business to Fitzgerald & Sons?

"Shannon? You all right?"

Ariel was at her side, looking concerned. Shannon had forgotten she'd be there despite the fact they'd spoken two days ago. Shannon wasn't surprised to see that her cousin had gone all out for her first meeting. She'd worn her hair down, swept into a Lauren Bacall bob that looked slinky and sophisticated. Her jacket was of a theme—big shoulders, fitted waist—as was her pencil skirt and five-inch heels. It worked.

"Shannon?"

"I'm fine," she said. "No problem finding the place?"

"None. And everyone's already been nice, although there's no chance I'll remember the names."

"I'll take you around. After." She held up the box of new cards. There weren't many brand-new ones, but there were a number of men for the taking. Some hadn't been chosen at all, though very few. Most had come back to the pile because that elusive piece of magic had been missing. Shannon had returned several cards of her own.

The room was relatively warm, no thanks to the inadequate radiator. They were lucky, though, that the church let them use the place to hold their exchange and in some cases cook their meals.

Long, rectangular tables had been set up in a circle of sorts, every participant had fourteen frozen containers stacked and ready to be distributed, waiting for the bagging portion of the afternoon.

For now, though, the women who were still seeking their special someone were gathered in front of Shannon's table. She put the box down as well as her heavy tote. "This is Ariel, everyone. I know she's met some of you, and in no time at all she'll be one of the regulars. She's a paralegal, smart as a whip and gorgeous, but you'll like her anyway. She's my cousin and she understands that we don't discuss the trading cards with outsiders. Lucky for us she's contributed a very attractive lawyer."

Her friends were smiling and shuffling closer, and she wondered if they could tell she wasn't herself. Part of her wished someone would take her aside, get her to spill all her woes. But while it was true she did consider most of these women true friends, they weren't like the girls she'd been close to in high school and college. Completely her fault. There had been ovations, invitations, phone calls. But for years now, the plant had been her life. The plant and her family.

Shannon began the ritual. She lifted the box of cards high, and the energy of the room expanded, a palpable spark. The box tilted and the cards fell into a gorgeous pile while the women dove in.

Only one pick was allowed each session. Only returned if there was no hope, or a one-night stand. How lucky were those guys? If they only knew. But sometimes the date turned into a relationship, and the one-night stand became a series of dates. In the two most famous cases, those one-night stands had turned into life-changing, living-together, monogamous relationships.

There they were, standing back by the kitchen itself, Bree Kingston and Rebecca Thorpe. They had become very close friends in the last two months. Bree was living with Charlie Winslow, owner and editor of the Naked New York media empire. Rebecca was responsible for that match because Charlie was her cousin. Then Rebecca had been rewarded with Jake.

Fairy-tale romances, both of them. The outcome every woman in the room prayed for.

And Shannon had forgotten to look for another card and now the pile had dwindled considerably. She sighed, not surprised. Things weren't going her way lately, so why should the trading cards be any different.

"I got him!" Ariel said, her voice an octave higher than normal.

"Who?" Shannon asked, her cousin's excitement infectious and fun.

"Nate. Your friend Nate. I had to fight for him, though. There were three of us who grabbed for the card but I was fastest. I told you I'd get him."

Shannon had to struggle to keep her smile, her composure. Ariel was going to go out with Nate. If he accepted… But of course he'd accept, why wouldn't he, especially because Shannon herself was going to set the date up.

"I can't wait to find out what he's got under that suit," Ariel said.

Shannon knew Ariel would be pleased. From the way the towel had draped, there was every reason to think Nate was fantastic all over.

Why had she thought this was a good idea? What kind of moron was she, thinking this would be the solution to her problem? As much as she liked Ariel, Shannon was seconds away from ripping the card from her hand and running for the hills.

He was hers, dammit.

Her breath stilled as a shudder ran down her back. He was hers? *Really?*

"Shannon? Something is wrong. You look terrible." Ariel put her hand on Shannon's arm. "I think you should sit down. Have some water."

Everyone hustled to make sure she was seated, that she had a fresh bottle of water, that she wasn't too warm or too cold. At least five palms pressed against her forehead. Which was sweet, it truly was.

What mattered most, though, was that she didn't cry. She wouldn't, because that's not what she did, not in front of people. Not because of a man she shouldn't be thinking about, not like *that*. She was tired, that's all. No breaks, no sleep, no answers.

Bree, pretty as a picture in her weird purple-and-orange dress, crouched down beside her. "Do you want me to call a taxi? Get you home?"

"No, thanks. I'm just tired. Insomnia. It's a bitch, but I'll get over it. I need to sit for a little while. Sip some water. Do you think you can get everyone back on track?"

"Absolutely. But I'll check with you again later, all right?"

"Thanks."

Bree squeezed her shoulder and Shannon relaxed as much as she could in the awful plastic chair, letting the commotion wash over her like a wave.

She'd set up the date between Nate and Ariel, she would. Just not right now.

THE SIXTH PROPERTY HAD seemed so good on paper, standing in the actual living room of the duplex made Nate's chest hurt. He'd been dreaming if he thought he could get a two-bedroom place for even a million. He turned to his Realtor, Aiko, and shook his head. "I know you warned me. Sorry I've wasted your time."

"It's no problem, Mr. Brennan. You needed to see what's happening for yourself. If you can believe it, this condo would have sold for twice what they're asking before the bubble burst."

"That's a terrifying thought." It wasn't as if it were filthy or had active rat colonies. The problem was the size. He'd lived in New York most of his life, and he'd thought he understood what that meant. But he'd been spoiled. His family home had been a relic, like the Fitzgeralds', only not as many floors. And not as much warmth, and the windows had been small even after the remodel. This condo looked as if they'd taken a moderately sized one-bedroom and split it into doll-sized rooms. He doubted either bedroom could hold more than a double bed, and that's with no other furniture included.

"Okay, so, what's next?"

Aiko smiled cheerfully, even though she had to be exhausted, hauling him all over hell and back looking at inappropriate buildings. "There's a nice condo in the Lower East Side you might really like."

"From now on, you lead the way." He glanced at his watch, surprised that it was after five. "I had no idea it was so late. We can reschedule."

"It's not a problem for me, if it's not a problem for you."

"Won't the building manager have an issue?"

"If I wanted to look at anything in this city at midnight, I wouldn't have a problem. But it's completely up to you."

He had a meeting with his attorney tomorrow, but not until eleven. There was one thing that he could do with, though. "One sec," he said, as he pulled out his cell.

Shannon answered on the first ring. "Hey," she said.

"Are you still at work?"

"Not at work, but working."

"Thinking of quitting anytime soon?"

"You read my thoughts," she said, sounding tired.

"I have a proposition. Meet me at a condo in the Lower East Side and I'll take you to dinner after. What do you think?"

She was quiet for so long he figured she'd beg off,

but then she said, "Where? I'm in Little Italy. If it's going to take me forever—"

"Hold on. I'm putting you on with Aiko. She has the address."

The women spoke as Nate rocked on his heels, anxious now to get to the new condo. Or maybe he was just anxious to see Shannon. He wanted her opinion. Her eyes. Hell, he wanted her.

6

SHANNON MET NATE AND AIKO in the lobby of a twenty-story building. The maintenance of the grounds, grass, shrubbery and trees was impressive, as was the location itself.

The Realtor, a pretty Asian woman in her early forties, was dressed impeccably and sensibly in heels that would merely hurt after a long day, not maim.

Nate looked wonderful. Very Euro in those crazy slim trousers that did wonders for his butt. Although, come to think of it, it was probably the other way around. A dark plum shirt tight enough that it stretched a tiny bit at the buttons. His black jacket was equally tailored and fit him like a glove. Oh, this had been such a bad idea.

"It's on the third floor," Aiko said, leading them to the elevator. After a quick ride they went to the farthest corner unit and she took them inside.

For its location alone, Shannon could see straight away that the unit was worth considering. It had low ceilings, standard in high-rise buildings that weren't off-the-charts expensive, as were the smallish rooms, but at least the living room would comfortably hold a couch and a couple of decent club chairs, and there was a fireplace. Gas, but ah, well.

"This is much better," Nate said.

Aiko then led them into the kitchen. It was a typical New York nightmare, everything crammed into the size of Shannon's mother's pantry. But the cabinetry wasn't bad, and neither was the flooring. Stainless-steel appliances. No task lighting, though. She'd seen professional chefs deal with less.

Aiko told them about the security, the gym, the laundry room, which was all fine, but the bedrooms had terrible closets, neither bathroom had a tub and, again, most of the lighting sucked. Still, there was natural light from two sides, which was a big deal. Depending on the price, he could do worse.

"It's seen some interest, but it's only been on the market for five days," Aiko said when they returned to the living room. "Why don't you think about it, and give me a call tomorrow. If you want to see more, we'll set up times then."

Nate smiled, put his hand on the small of Shannon's back and escorted both women to the door.

Shannon was absolutely, completely certain that he had not only felt the electrical jolt that had scorched through her at his touch, but could also sense the full-body blush that was going to set her on fire if he continued to let his thumb make little circles on her blouse.

She didn't breathe much on the way down, letting out a loud gush of air as Nate stepped away to shake hands with Aiko.

"It was nice meeting you," she said.

Shannon made some sort of sound, cleared her throat and somehow managed to say, "You, too. Have a good evening."

Nate turned to Shannon and narrowed his eyes. "I was thinking Katz's."

"Katz's sounds great."

He held the door open for her, but didn't touch her as they left the building. She would tell him about Ariel the moment they sat down at the deli. He'd be delighted. Why wouldn't he be delighted? Ariel was great. Pretty. Shannon had a picture of her on her cell so she could show him. It would be done in a flash, then she'd have the matzo ball soup, and they'd talk real estate. She knew a lot about real estate.

"I'll warn you right now, I'm ordering all the stuff I can't get in Indonesia. A knish, latkes, kishke, the works." He grinned.

They walked to the curb, where they waited to get a cab, as several, occupied, drove by. It was dinner hour and it would be nuts at the deli, but that was okay, because she was going to set up the date with Ariel first thing, then it would become easy. Simple. Eating good things, talking square footage and hardwood floors.

Finally, an empty cab stopped in front of them. Nate opened the door, and she jumped inside, grabbing the door handle in a panic. "You know what, I forgot. I'm supposed to be... I'm sorry, I have to... I'll see you at the— Sorry." Then she slammed the door shut and pretty much screamed her address at the cabby.

"WHAT THE HELL WAS THAT?" Nate said, to no one in particular. Stunned, he watched the taxi weave into the bumper-to-bumper traffic as he tried to interpret the past few minutes.

He was certain she hadn't forgotten anything. Unless the thing she'd forgotten was hugely embarrassing, but that seemed unlikely.

Had he said something out of line before the deli talk? He reran the evening as nearly as he could remember and nothing jumped out at him. Nothing even whispered vaguely. Everything had been fine, then whoosh, she was out of there like a shot, and her cheeks had burned pink, and he was utterly bewildered.

He debated going after her, but he doubted she wanted to be chased. So he raised his arm and flagged down another cab, too dazed to care about how long it took.

The wait at the deli was even longer. He tried to think about the condo, then about tomorrow's meeting with the attorney, but each thought was hijacked by Shannon. He gave in and picked up one of the free papers at the door and turned to the classified section. It wasn't very big, and most of it was for rentals and rent shares.

It kept him occupied for a couple of minutes while he stood in line, but then thoughts of Shannon returned to bedevil him. He wasn't dim about women. He had enough empirical evidence to prove it. He was perfectly capable of picking up signals, and ever since the wedding, he and Shannon had definitely been signaling. Which was complicated because—

"Oh," he said aloud, gaining the attention of the older woman in front of him. He smiled briefly, then went back to his revelation.

She'd left because of the signals. The heat between them.

No, wait, that wasn't quite right. She'd run because of the complications that came along with the heat between them. Now everything was falling into place. He sighed, and it must have been a hell of a sigh because the same older woman put her hand on the back of her hair, turned and gave him a very disgruntled glare.

He smiled again, dismissed the notion of apologizing and went back to his theory. Luckily, the unhappy woman and her group were led to a table, and a few minutes later he was sitting in a small booth underneath a wall of framed celebrity photographs, staring at a large menu.

Since he already knew what he was having, he waited impatiently for someone to take his order, asking preemptively for take-out containers, then, with his Dr. Brown's Cream Soda crackling over ice, he pulled out his cell phone.

He turned it so he could text, then thought for a moment before he decided to keep things light and easy. No reason to stir the pot yet.

I can order an extra knish if you want. Maybe some chopped liver?

Nate smiled at that. Shannon hated liver in any guise. As the seconds ticked by, his smile faded. He probably shouldn't have texted her. She'd left because she was uncomfortable, and he could only guess at the why. That whole signal thing? Was that just wishful thinking on his part? He got all hot and bothered when he touched her, or saw her, or thought of her, but she might not feel a thing.

Maybe *he* was making her uncomfortable, not the complications. She'd come to see the condo tonight because she felt obligated. He was Danny's best friend, practically part of their family. Of course she'd agree to come help him find a place. She wanted him out of the house. Her house. Jesus, what had he—

His phone beeped, notifying him of an incoming text. He clicked it so fast he almost dropped the phone.

Thanks, but that's ok. Sorry I ran off.

Don't worry about it. Stuff happens.

It was rude. I wanted to ask you something.

I'm all ears. Or eyes, I suppose.

Nate tensed. He felt it from his neck to his calves. It didn't make a lot of sense, considering she was probably going to ask him something completely innocuous.

U interested in dating while you're in town?

Dating? She was asking him on a date? On the cell phone? So he'd been right. It was about the signals. He'd known it, dammit. Things didn't get that hot between two people without both of them knowing. Especially when one of them had worn nothing but a towel and a rising hard-on. But he still had to play it cool. It would be a damn shame to scare her off now.

Sure. What did u have in mind?

He sipped his soda as he waited. And waited. It must be one hell of a long text because she was taking her sweet time. His food came, and he kept watching the phone as the waitress arranged the big plates on the small table. Finally, another ding.

He was back to tense in a second, only this time it was with eager anticipation.

My cousin Ariel met u at the wedding. She'd like to meet u for drinks tmrow nite at Molly's. She's great. Pretty. You'll like her.

The breath he'd been holding rushed out of him, smothering the spark starting to flame. He didn't remember meeting anyone named Ariel at the wedding. He had no interest in going for drinks with Shannon's cousin. How the hell had he gotten things so screwed up?

Sure. Send me her #. I'll call.

His typing was slow, each word a punch to his gut. It wasn't easy to press Send, but he did.

The pause that followed gave him enough time to realize the containers the waitress had brought weren't going to be sufficient. His hunger had vanished, and while he wanted to walk out and leave it all behind, he wasn't going to. That would be ridiculous. Shannon wasn't intentionally hurting him. There was nothing between them, couldn't be anything between them. Any interest he'd experienced had been one-sided. It happened. Not to him, not before now, and that was why he was caught off guard. Hell, he was just her brother's friend, that's all.

In fact, what she was doing was something friends did. It was nice of her to set him up. A few dates would keep him from getting bored as he waited to get back to his real home.

The beep sounded, and he hoped it wasn't her saying goodbye.

It was.

SHANNON KNEW HE WAS HOME. Not because she'd heard
him—the one thing this old brownstone had was excellent soundproofing as long as there weren't connecting
walls. No, for some reason she couldn't fathom, Danny
had knocked on her damn door and announced Nate's
arrival. At least her brother hadn't opened the door. He
knew better. But she especially didn't want Nate to see
her like this. In her flannel nightgown, scrunched under
her covers, TV on some show she didn't care about, her
laptop open on some website on marketing she hadn't
bothered to read and a big bowl of Kraft's blue box
of macaroni and cheese in her hands, the alarmingly
orange pasta being devoured as quickly as she could
shove the spoonfuls in her mouth.

She hummed a bar of "I Feel Pretty" then sagged
against her pillows. How had her life come to this? And
why, *why* was the nonstarter with Nate the thing that
was crushing her chest?

It must be transference. Better to obsess about a guy
than the very real fear that she couldn't save the plant.
That no matter how many times she thought things
would be okay, that the family would move on, that the
struggle to hold on to a building and a brownstone when
they were worth enough that her whole family could be
secure for the rest of their lives was idiotic....

Yes, better to think about a guy, when the truth was,
she couldn't let the business go. Everything in her believed in holding on. That what her family had was pre-
cious and worth keeping, and that money—even barrels
of money—was no replacement for the legacy, the lessons, the heart and soul generations had dedicated to
this life.

Maybe her crush—and was there ever a more appropriate word?—on Nate was another way to cling to

her past. It probably had nothing to do with the man he was now. But what he represented. Continuity. Treasured memories.

She put the almost empty bowl on her nightstand, wanting to weep. She should never have taken those psychology classes at City College.

Finding the remote, she clicked off the TV, then logged off her computer and slipped it under her bed. One click and the room fell dark, except for the alarm clock that mocked her with it's big red 8:30. She'd never fall asleep this early. Or at all. It was ludicrous to try, but she shut her eyes anyway.

She had no idea what she was going to do tomorrow. How she was going to face Nate. She was a decent actress, but no one was that good. He'd see too much if he got a look at her. Pain, lust, jealousy, sadness. Or maybe that had just been her when she'd looked in the mirror before climbing into bed.

Ariel was a nice person. Nate was, too. And if they slept together, Shannon would shatter like spun glass rolling off a table.

It didn't matter that he'd never be hers, that wanting him made no sense at all, that she was being ridiculous. She didn't even know him well enough to like him this much.

Hmm. Maybe she'd gotten it backward, and it would be easier to think about the business closing down. At least that sadness made some sense.

A SPLASH OF LIGHT ACROSS her eyes woke Shannon with a start. She was shocked she'd fallen asleep at all, let alone 'til morning. But there was no denying the very loud buzzing of her alarm, which she ended as quickly as she could.

Her eyes felt gummy and her mouth awful. Ah, she hadn't brushed her teeth. She never went to sleep without brushing her teeth. And, if the evidence were to be believed, she'd wept.

She ought to have remembered that part, no? Given the state of her bed, there'd been lots of tossing and turning. Regardless, it was past 6:00 a.m. and she wanted to make it out of the shower in record time. She planned on grabbing a bite to eat on the way to work, and if the coffee wasn't ready, she'd buy a cup, too, even though it was a terrible waste of money.

What mattered was leaving the house before she had to face Nate. She should stay, show him Ariel's picture, talk her cousin up, smile, act like the friend she was pretending to be. But not with puffy eyes. Not this early. She'd send him the photo. That's what cell phones were made for. Sort of.

Didn't matter, she was out of bed, had her clothing ready to go, her robe on, and she practically ran to the bathroom. The lock clicking into place was a very welcome sound, and the hot water pouring over her eased some of the tension that had become a regular part of her life. At this rate, she'd have an ulcer by thirty.

She didn't waste another moment, though, and went through her routine double time. She was glad the mirror was fogged, because she needed to prepare to face herself. Maybe she wouldn't turn on the lights on her bedroom vanity. No, that wouldn't work. She needed the makeup too much.

As soon as she made it back to her room, she got dressed, got her iPod out and set it to shuffle. Then she turned that sucker up loud. She planned on listening all the way to the plant and only when her workday began would she let herself think a single thought.

It was an extremely effective technique up until the moment she bumped into Nate in the kitchen.

"Sorry," he said.

She didn't hear him say it but even she could read those lips. Tempted to throw up her hands and run, after a moment's thought, she put the idea aside. She'd have to face him sooner or later, so why not now? The silence when she turned off the music was profound.

"You okay?"

She made a small production of taking out the earbuds. "Didn't know you were here."

"So I imagine. You must be pretty serious about your musicals to listen that loud."

"Musicals are important."

"So's your hearing."

"Thank you, Doctor, I'll take it under advisement."

He raised a sardonic brow. "I was getting some coffee."

The empty mug in his hand had clued her in, but her snarky comeback stalled in her throat as she got a load of him in his pajamas. Spider-Man had been replaced by out-and-out elegance. They were glen plaid, with blue piping, covered by a plush white robe, like something she'd expect to see in the movies, not in their brownstone. The sartorial splendor was damn near dazzling. T-shirts and boxers were the ongoing trend with her brothers, and her father was a flannel man all the way. Nate looked sharp. Sexy.

Shannon went for the cupboard with the mugs before things got out of control. More out of control.

"You gonna take a lunch to work?" Nate asked.

"I hadn't thought about it," she said, busy, very, very busy with her to-go cup.

"I could put something together, if you want. I was

kidding about the chopped liver. I wouldn't do that to you."

She tried to laugh, but had to switch to a cough midway. "Nice of you to remember."

"Nice of you to set me up with your friend."

"Cousin."

"Right. Cousin. Ariel, is it?"

"Yep." She kept her voice peppy. Making sure to smile as she said the word. That really did work.

"I've tried, but I don't remember her from the wedding."

"There were so many people there." Shannon filled her cup from the big old urn, then focused on stirring.

"I stopped noticing after I saw you."

Her spoon stilled. Her heart raced. She didn't dare look up. If she looked at him, she was going to fold. She would confess to everything, even if she didn't know what she was confessing about. One look, and she would get herself into a mess she wouldn't be able to get out of.

Instead she laughed. The smile trick worked with laughter, too. Well enough, at least. "You were just surprised I wasn't wearing a tiara." She kept her head down as she went to the sink. "I've got to dash, but—"

Shannon glanced up. It was a mistake, a reflex, but Nate was standing right there, directly in her line of sight, and the way he was looking at her stopped her midsentence.

She felt a punch to her heart, an ache of need and want and *please.* But only for a second. "I'll send you her picture," she said, turning away, pulling down the curtain. "You guys will have a great time, I know it."

But she got the hell out of the kitchen. Fast. She put on her coat, grabbed her purse and her briefcase and she was out the door. It occurred to her as she reached the subway that it would have looked more natural if she'd said goodbye.

No matter. She'd let down her guard for only an instant. He'd probably thought she'd been making a face about her coffee.

7

AT TWO-THIRTY, NATE CAUGHT a cab and told the driver to take him to Fitzgerald & Sons. He hadn't been there since high school, but that didn't matter, he knew the address. It was a huge building, half a block long, and the smell of it—hot-melt glue and the emulsion they used for the lithography—was unforgettable. The noise was crippling, and he and Danny had been under a mandatory earplug rule.

As the cab inched its way through the omnipresent traffic, he made a couple of phone calls, then spun the phone around for texting.

Where are U?

She might not answer him. She'd know the text was his, and she could just not reply and he'd never know if she had turned her cell off for a meeting, or left it in her desk, or if she'd glanced at his name and thought nothing of putting the phone away. But he stared at his screen anyway.

Three very long, slow blocks later, the phone beeped.

At the plant. Why?

U real busy?

Just the usual...

Mind if I stop by?

Anytime. I'll be here.

Nate clicked out of his phone and put it in his coat pocket. He'd have been in trouble if she'd told him she wasn't busy. That hadn't been likely, though. According to Danny, according to everyone who knew Shannon, she was in perpetual motion, if not working on marketing for the plant, then putting together some special event at the church or at a park or coordinating a fundraiser for something or other.

Everyone who lived between Midtown and SoHo knew Shannon Fitzgerald. It wasn't a surprise she edited the online Gramercy newsletter. She wasn't involved with the kid pageants anymore, but she did help out with an amateur theater group and a dance studio. Danny hadn't told him that. Mrs. Fitz had. In fact, Mrs. Fitz had a hell of a lot to say about her only daughter.

None of it had been unkind. Shannon was a blessing to the family, but she was working too hard, doing too much, and for what? Mrs. Fitz had sprayed cabbage soup across the kitchen counter as she waved her spoon during that discourse. Nate had picked up a sponge and followed her around, nodding when appropriate and smiling at how Mrs. Fitz hadn't changed a bit.

Shannon had, though. He couldn't think of her anymore as that child he'd known. The pictures of her back then had been replaced by current images, mental snapshots he'd collected since the wedding.

The best part of New York so far? Mornings over coffee, when Shannon was there. Molly's, with her laughter high and sweet over the noise of the crowd.

He'd spent today with attorneys, nitpicking their way through a contract so complicated it made his head spin. He'd had enough of maneuvering and tricky language. Ever since Shannon had bowled him backward with that look this morning, he'd had a low-grade fever that needed attention. He'd felt as if he'd seen her naked. Want had been clear as day in her eyes, and her heat had singed him from across the room.

She was at the plant. Being four blocks away, if the traffic didn't ease up, he was gonna get out of the cab and walk. Because he needed to know what the hell. That's all. Just what the hell.

SHANNON LOOKED UP AT BRADY, who'd stopped talking. Shouting, actually, as they were on the floor of the plant and the noise was ridiculous with three of their biggest machines running. He wasn't even looking at her, and he seemed surprised.

She turned, expecting to see Nate, but not the effect he'd have on her.

Her whole body reacted. Heat raced up her neck and into her cheeks, her heart could have jump-started a stalled car, and even the small hairs at her nape stood as pure adrenaline replaced all the blood in her veins.

He knew. He knew that she wanted him, that it was killing her to give him to Ariel. He'd seen it this morning, maybe before this morning. He knew she wanted him, and that she thought of him naked, and that she'd masturbated twice while she'd pictured him, and oh,

God, maybe she'd blurted out something in her sleep and he'd heard her because the wall was so thin, and now he was coming to tell her to stop. To leave him alone. To quit thinking of him as anything but a friend of the family; for God's sake, what was she, some kind of animal who couldn't control herself?

Even the pounding of the pressrun and the offset rollers couldn't compete with the hammering in her heart as Nate approached. He nodded at Brady, then caught her eye.

She knew she should smile. It was only polite. She managed a delayed blink instead.

He pointed to the offices—to her office—and she stumbled forward, got her feet steady and led him, squeezing her hands into tight fists until she held her door open, waiting for him.

As he passed, his hand brushed the back of hers, the clenching hand flexing open, reaching, but for only a second. She closed the door, automatically pulling out her earplugs and dropping them in the small ceramic bowl she used only for that purpose.

Nate slipped his coat off, hung it on the hook on the back of the door. She used the time to move behind her desk. When he turned to face her, he seemed disconcerted that she'd crossed the room so quickly.

"You know, I think I recognized a couple of people out there," he said. "Discounting Brady. But it's been years since my last visit. I was in high school, I think, working that summer before I went to NYU."

"That makes sense. Some of our employees have been with us over twenty years."

"I seem to remember there were more of them."

She wet her bottom lip, wished she had a bottle of water in the office as her throat felt parched. "We've had to downsize. Like most of the businesses around here. It's tough out there these days."

He took a couple of steps, but didn't head for a chair.

She wasn't sure if he was waiting for her to sit first or— "What are you doing here?"

He got that startled look again. Eyes widened, lips parted, a tiny little jerk of his head. Then he smiled, and he went back to looking like regular Nate. Calm, confident, as if he knew something she didn't. "I was hoping to talk for a few minutes, if that's okay with you."

All she had to do was say no. That she was due in a meeting, that it wasn't a good time. Then she remembered his text, and her response.

"Well, it depends what you need because I'm not off-the-clock yet. But I did think that condo was a good deal."

"I'm not here about real estate," he said, taking yet another step.

She pulled her office chair closer, as if the desk weren't enough of a barrier. "I don't understand."

"I've canceled my date with Ariel," he said. "I thought you should know."

Shannon hadn't expected that. Not even a little. "Why?"

Nate grinned again. "I hope it doesn't make things uncomfortable between the two of you. It was nothing to do with her. I told her that, and I think she was fine. It wasn't as if there was much for her to be disappointed about."

"What are you talking about?" Shannon stepped away from the chair and rounded her desk. "You're great looking, you work for Architects Without Borders or whatever, but the bottom line is you're a hero who is helping all kinds of people who've just gone through the worst thing living can throw at them, and you're funny. Not how you used to be—you and Danny, God, you were awful when you were kids with all that bathroom humor—but now there's wit there which I wish I could say about my brother. So don't go saying you're not much, because that's not true at all. She'd be lucky to go out with you."

Nate's stare was a mix of wonder and bewilderment, at least that's what it looked like from her end. She had gotten carried away a little, but it was because she was nervous, and when she got nervous things got jumbled if she didn't have a script or a routine or prepared answers to questions she'd been asked a hundred times.

"I meant," he said carefully, "because we didn't know each other. Me and Ariel. For all she knew I could be the worst date in New York. I don't think I am, but that's pretty subjective."

She inhaled. Exhaled. Stared at his hazel eyes, at the gentleness of his smile. He had great teeth, just great. White and even, and his lips, they were exactly the right size for his face. He was really good-looking, but in a nonthreatening way. He didn't beat you over the head with it. In fact, he made her relax, when she wasn't being an idiot and thinking about what his body looked like under that suit. "Well, okay, then. Thanks for telling me." She turned, walked back around the desk and pulled the chair in front of her once more.

NATE BURST OUT LAUGHING, BUT caught it fast with a quick fake cough covered by his hand. But damn, it was hard not to just let go. His head had been spinning since the minute he'd seen Shannon's face when he'd walked into the plant. She'd seemed paralyzed and frantic at the same time. He couldn't hear shit, but maybe that had made him notice the way her eyes got huge and her breathing quickened, and how she looked like she was waiting for the starting gun to go off.

The fists had made him doubt the wisdom in coming to see her. He never wanted to make her anxious, and if clenching her hands so tightly her knuckles paled wasn't a sign of anxiety, he didn't know what was.

The big giant question was what she wanted to run from. Him? Had he said something horrendous and not known it? Did something happen between the condo and the taxicab that had fundamentally changed her attitude toward him? Maybe it was a memory, an awful thing he'd done as a kid that she'd repressed until the moment he'd mentioned knishes.

But if she suddenly had realized he was someone to run from, what the hell was all that about his being a hero, and how he was great looking—

She thought he was great looking. That was cool. It wasn't what he lived for, but it was nice to hear, especially when she was such a knockout.

It didn't matter. Because knockout or not, he couldn't do anything about it until he understood what her deal was. He waited until she was looking at him again, and when their gazes met, he said, "What's going on, Shannon?"

She froze again. "What do you mean?"

"The cab yesterday. This morning. Have I done something? Said something to offend you?"

"No!" she said, way too loudly for the room. About an octave too high, as well. "No, don't be silly." Her cheeks had started to get pink and as she kept looking at anything but him, plucking at the top of her chair, moving sideways, away, a quarter-inch at a time— "Of course not."

Nate turned his head, looked behind him, expecting a person, a camera, something that would explain this completely insane sketch-comedy routine of hers. As far as he could tell, it was the two of them, alone, and she'd gone off her rocker.

"Did you want coffee?" she asked, brightly. "I think we have doughnuts left, but they won't be the good ones. Nothing cream-filled or glazed. Everyone goes for those first."

"Nope, I'm good," he said.

"So no coffee?"

"No, thanks."

She continued to pluck at the back of her chair. Gave him a disarming smile when the time had stretched past the awkward stage. "Tea?"

"Shannon. Please? You're my…" He hesitated, uncertain what to call her. "I admit we weren't very close when we were kids, but we're not kids anymore, and I've enjoyed talking to you. Getting to know you now. As a friend." He stepped a little closer, afraid if he moved too far too fast, he'd spook her and she really would make a run for it. "As a woman. The other night at Molly's, that was a good time, wasn't it? And in the mornings when we've had coffee? I mean, you came to the rescue yesterday about the condo, and then, I don't even know what happened. I must have upset you somehow, and if I did, I'm sorry. It wasn't intentional."

"You didn't."

Her voice was so low he wasn't completely sure he'd heard right. "What?"

"You didn't. Upset me."

"Then why am I making you so nervous? I don't understand."

She looked so uncomfortable, it made him want to

do whatever it took to relax her. But he had no jokes at the ready, nothing, in fact, that would change things. Except to leave, and he wasn't going to do that. It would drive him insane for this to continue, to not know. If it truly was his interest in her that was at the heart of things, he'd stop. He wasn't sure how, but he would. He wouldn't let himself linger over thoughts of her, would turn away when all he wanted to do was drink her in like champagne.

"It's not you," she said, and then it seemed as if she were going to explain everything. But she didn't. Instead she lowered her head a fraction. "It's work. There are so many people doing their own printing now, and we've had to make adjustments. The employees are having a difficult time. We've had to end the medical plan here, which is a blow to everyone. But it was bleeding us dry. I'm going to get new customers, though. Before you know it, we'll be right back to full capacity. In fact, I'm meeting with a rep from Carnation foods. Printing can labels is a very lucrative market that we never pursued. And then there's print-on-demand for novels, that's a whole new field."

He didn't believe her. Not that the plant was having financial difficulties, that was to be expected. But what was going on between the two of them had nothing to do with her job. "And that's what freaked you out on the street? When you jumped in the cab? Right that minute, you realized things were hard at work?"

The pink in her cheeks remained steady, but Shannon turned her body to the right, as if she were going to move to the big filing cabinet that stood in the corner. "No, not right that second."

"Shannon? I…"

Her shoulders rose then fell, and she turned to face

him, her smile not nearly reaching her eyes. "I should really get back to work."

"Right," he said. He wanted to kick the chair he hadn't taken. He'd never been in a situation like this before. But he couldn't see how he could force her into telling him the truth. Then a thought hit him, and he grew concerned. "You're all right? You're not sick or anything?"

"No. I'm fine. There's nothing wrong, Nate. I'm sorry my behavior seems erratic, but I've always been weird. I've heard you call me that enough times."

"That was different. You and your tiaras."

"I was a little kid," she said. "With four big brothers who liked nothing more than tormenting me and making my life a living hell. And you were no better."

"I'm sorry about that. Princess."

"Hey," she said, and for the first time since last night she smiled at him for real. "It was more my mother's idea than mine."

"You loved it, though. Being on stage, doing all that twirling around. Singing and posing."

She nodded. "I did."

"By the time I was old enough to appreciate your talents, I was too busy going through puberty to pay attention. I'm sorry about that, too."

"You didn't miss all that much."

"I think I missed a great deal," he said, and his voice had gone low and rough as he moved right next to her massive wooden desk.

There it was again. The look from this morning. Raw and real and there was no way he was getting this wrong. He rounded the desk and shoved her damn chair right back into the wall. Her head tilted up, and her pink lips parted.

He took hold of her arms and pulled her into a kiss that blocked out every single thing but the taste, the feel and the scent of Shannon Fitzgerald.

8

SHANNON STOPPED. STOPPED breathing, moving, thinking. His lips. Her lips. Together. Kissing. *Oh.*

Then his tongue, the tip of his tongue, slipped over her bottom lip, and sparks shot through her like fireworks, and she gave up, gave in. Her hands went to his hips, under his jacket, and she steadied herself as she touched him, as she parted her lips and took what he offered.

Thinking would come later. Now was for goose bumps and heat. She'd wanted this so much, and even if she had to stop, because at some point they'd have to, she wouldn't have to give this back.

Nothing between them could go beyond the press of his mouth and the slide of her tongue, but she could have the memory and that was something.

She felt him pull back, and maybe it was just to breathe, or to change his angle, but what if it wasn't? She followed him, leaning forward, chasing him. It couldn't be over, not yet, not when they may not ever...

His breath on her lips and her chin, the loss, made her open her eyes. He was still close, still gripping her arms, but he looked startled, as if he weren't sure how he'd ended up in this kiss. Not sorry, though. Smiling. As if he might laugh or shout, and it wasn't at all a surprise when he looked around the office for a second or two, because she needed to get her bearings, too.

He came back to her, though. His smile settled down, his eyes darkened, and he stared at her. His right hand floated near her face before his fingertips brushed the path of her blush up her cheek to her temple. "You're so beautiful," he said, then winced slightly. "More than beautiful. How did that happen? When?"

"You went away."

"And you became a gorgeous woman."

She doubted she could blush harder. "You came back better, too."

"Older, at least." His fingers moved through her hair, carefully, slowly. "Hopefully wiser."

"Definitely better," she said, momentarily panicked that wiser meant he knew they shouldn't be doing this.

"I don't want to stop."

She stepped closer to him, letting more of her body press against his. "No one's asking you to."

"But—"

"Not yet," she whispered as her eyes were closing. "Please."

"No, not yet," he repeated before he kissed her again.

It didn't seem possible, but the second kiss was better. She could feel how she affected him, and not only by the passion of his kiss, the slide of his tongue, but also by the pressure on her hip from his burgeoning arousal.

"Shannon," he whispered as he pulled back, then his mouth was on hers again, as if that tiny distance had been too much to handle.

His hands had grown as possessive as his lips, running over her shoulders, her back, the curve of her bottom.

She smiled against his mouth, right in the middle of the kiss. Then she pushed her hips forward. Nothing major, not a bump or a grind, just a yes, permission to move again, to keep stealing her breath with his desire.

How she wished there weren't all these clothes between them. She had been aching to touch his bare chest since that moment in the—

A knock on her door made her gasp and jump back as if it had been a gunshot.

Somehow Nate was a good foot away from her, his eyes panicked. She had the feeling she appeared as guilty as he did. Fortunately for her, she didn't have an obvious erection to worry about. "Sit down," she said.

He nodded, went around her desk. Sitting wasn't enough, he had to cross his legs.

She pulled her chair back, then ran her hands down her blazer and slacks. She exhaled, hoping like hell she wasn't as red as a beet as she opened the door.

Brady barely glanced at her. "I could use your help," he said, then turned and headed back to the floor.

Shannon closed the door, leaned her head against it and tried to catch her breath.

"I'll go in a minute," Nate said.

"Okay," she said. "Thanks for…"

He cleared his throat. "I'll see you later."

She left her office, remembering at the last second to take her earplugs with her.

All she could think was that she'd just made the biggest mistake ever. How was it possible to feel like this after one kiss?

Two hours later Nate still couldn't stop thinking about the kiss. He hadn't planned it. If he had it wouldn't have happened in her office with dozens of people around. But then maybe that had been a good thing. Or else he doubted he could've stopped. They both sure as hell had some thinking to do.

He came up on an old haunt of his and Danny's—the basketball court three blocks down from the Fitzgeralds'—amazed that at this time of day it wasn't jammed with kids. He couldn't remember ever finding the place empty. It didn't make sense, until he climbed over the fence and almost broke his neck landing on a crack in the asphalt.

The court was situated in a corner field belonging to a family who owned a bunch of drugstores. They'd turned it into a basketball court, put in lights for night games, built risers, made it nice. There'd been never-ending graffiti on the two walls, and the big fence had gone up when Nate had been fourteen. But everyone in the neighborhood played there. Kept things civil.

Guess the goodwill had run out. Or maybe a basketball court didn't mean all that much when people were having trouble feeding their families. It still made him sad, and he debated chucking it in and going to Molly's for a beer instead.

What the hell. It was a Friday at four-thirty, so maybe he'd shoot some hoops, see if he could get a game of one-on-one. If not, he'd still burn up some energy. He'd always done his best thinking while sweating.

He tossed his jacket on a low riser, grateful he'd brought the basketball he'd found in Myles's room. Dribbling took on a whole new dimension as he zigzagged to miss the cracks and gouges. At least the hoop was still in play, even if the backboard was half-gone.

He stood where he imagined the free-throw line was, shot and missed. That wasn't a big surprise. He hadn't played in a long time.

In Bali, where he stayed between jobs, he did a lot of kayaking and swimming, and the gym he belonged to didn't have a court. He got more practice shooting pool than hoops, which was a shame. He loved the game even though he wasn't that great at it.

With hardly any backboard left, he had to run after every other shot, and even though the temperature was cool he worked up a sweat pretty quickly. But as time passed he began to hit a little more often than he missed.

Although he couldn't afford not to pay attention to where he was running, he still had enough concentration left over to think about Shannon.

Damn, he hoped things didn't get weird between them.

He had no idea what he'd expected. To take her right there on her big old desk? That they would rush back to her parents' home and go at it in her bedroom with Mr. and Mrs. Fitz downstairs and the TV blaring from the family room?

None of the reasons that being with Shannon was a bad idea had disappeared. He was a guest in the family home. He supposed he could move back to the hotel, but he hated that idea.

He had to really think this through. Yeah, he wanted her something fierce, but he wasn't going to be in New York for long. Shannon didn't strike him as a casual sex kind of woman. Besides, he wasn't feeling particularly casual about her. Casual meant that each of them were mostly out for themselves. Not a bad thing when it was mutual, but Nate cared about the possible fallout.

Danny had mentioned that Shannon was looking for something real, for something that would last. She wasn't sitting in an ivory tower waiting, but she was particular about her choices.

He wouldn't be anyone's choice, especially someone like Shannon. She'd never want his kind of life. He couldn't picture her in Bali, not the Bali he knew. He wasn't living with the expats or hanging out with the spa retreat crowd. He lived on the cheap, in a shack near the beach. The electricity was spotty at best, the plumbing wasn't much better, and he slept in the raw under a mosquito net.

A friend of his, an expat from England into real estate, kept a room for him in his South Bali cliffside villa, which was where Nate stored his clothing and anything of value, but as he spent so much time in inhospitable areas where the only shoes he needed were flip-flops or his heavy work boots, he didn't visit it often.

Shannon was a villa woman all the way.

She was also someone he liked a great deal, and sex complicated things. He might not want to live in Manhattan, but when he did come to visit, there was no place he'd rather be welcomed than the Fitzgeralds'. He'd hate it if he messed things up with her, with them.

Weirdly, though, he wasn't interested in anyone else. It didn't seem to matter that sleeping with Shannon was off the table, he'd rather spend his evenings with her than any other woman in New York.

Good thing he was well versed in the single palm arts.

He threw the basketball entirely too hard. It flew back to the shadowy section of the court. He hadn't noticed it was getting so late. Time flew when a guy was realizing he wasn't going to get laid for at least a month.

Wiping his face with his T-shirt, he headed for the

ball, and when he bent to get it, he heard a very distinc-
tive voice.

"My ma says you better get home right this minute,
Nate Brenner. She didn't slave all day over corned beef
and cabbage so that you could be out here playing with
yourself."

He grinned through his wince. The speech had
been almost verbatim from back in the day. Only he'd
been out here with Danny, and Shannon had never said
that last bit. He was glad she had now. Guess things
wouldn't be weird between them.

"Tell her to keep her shirt on," he said, which was
something Danny had shouted more often than not.
"I'm coming." Nate stood, and there she was, outside
the gate. She had her hands stuffed in her coat pockets, and the last rays of the sun were showing off in her
hair, making her look like something created by magic.
As he walked toward her, his grin got bigger with each
step.

"How'd you know I was here?" he asked.

"Mom saw you leave with the basketball."

"I didn't see her."

"She's good at that."

"Stealth Mom."

"I think it comes with the territory. Especially with
four boys."

"What," he said, standing inches away, watching her
through the wire fence, relieved there was no awkward-
ness, no averting of gazes, "you don't think she had to
keep her eye on you?"

Shannon shook her head. "I was the Princess, remember? I got off on being perfect."

"Sounds excruciating."

"It was. Certainly no fun."

"There's still time to make up for that," he said. "Catch." He tossed the ball over the fence and she caught it easily. After grabbing his jacket, he started climbing, jumping down on the other side a little too soon. He jarred his neck and cursed his vanity.

"I'm not good at getting into trouble. Not enough practice." She slid him a look he couldn't interpret, but something about it got his cock's attention.

"Good thing you're friends with a master, then," he said, studying her reaction.

"A master, huh?"

He slipped on his jacket, his mind racing. So neither of them was bringing up the kiss. Not overtly, anyway. Trouble was he had no idea what that meant. That they were going to pretend it never happened? Or pick up where they left off as soon as humanly possible? His body emphatically voted for the latter, but his head warned him to watch his step.

"You coming?" she asked. She'd taken a few steps toward home and he hadn't noticed.

He decided to test the water. Put a toe in, nothing too drastic. He caught up with her. "After dinner, you want to do something?"

She looked at him, eyes narrowed, and if he had to guess he would say that she was testing the water, as well. "What did you have in mind?"

"It's obvious you've missed out on a large part of your education. It's a moral imperative that I corrupt you to make up for the lack. We could start with stealing a candy bar at the Duane Reade."

"No." She laughed the word more than said it. "I'm not going to steal things from the drugstore. Jeez."

"Ah," he said, as they walked very slowly, "a challenge. Which is fine. I'd be disappointed if you made this too easy."

"And there'll be no cherry bombs in toilets, or toilet paper wrapped around trees, or crank phone calls, either."

"Those are classics for a reason." Her laughter made him ridiculously happy. "You don't have to work tomorrow, right?"

"I don't have to, but I'm going to. I have to make a million Easter baskets."

"A million?"

"Give or take."

"Okay, so that means I can get you drunk, but not epically hungover."

A big man walking a tiny little dog shared their sidewalk for a moment, forcing Shannon's right side against Nate's left. When the coast was clear, they didn't shift back. "I don't like being drunk," she said.

"I'm beginning to see why you aren't very good at getting into trouble."

"I don't think you were drunk every time you got sent to the principal's office."

"Not *every* time, no." He turned to find her grinning up at him.

"I don't like to be drunk because I don't like to miss things," she said. "Especially not wonderful things. I want to be where I am and remember what I've done."

"You think getting into trouble with me would be wonderful?"

"Not a doubt in my mind."

They had slowed down so much they were barely walking. They'd reached the steps of the house, cars continued to zoom past, the night had finally come to stay. She stood in a pool of lamplight, and he couldn't hold off any longer.

He had to kiss her.

SHANNON KEPT HER GRIP ON the stupid ball under her arm, even though she wanted to pull Nate closer. She'd wanted to kiss him again, but it had seemed like a bad idea. She'd been right. They were standing in front of her house, for goodness' sakes. He was a master at getting in trouble.

Unencumbered by basketballs or good sense, Nate found the perfect angle, and his lips warmed quickly in the night air. Actual breathing was thrown out in favor of not stopping at all, just learning new ways to make the parts that mattered light up with sensation and need.

A honk blew it straight to hell. She jerked back, he tried to push her behind him in some kind of caveman-ish gesture of protection, and the kids honked again, shouting lewd things out the window of their car.

"Well, that sucked," Nate said.

Shannon shoved the ball at him until he took it. "I'll see you at the dinner table." She didn't even glance at him as she ran up the stairs. It probably would have been more polite to hold the door for him, but she let it slam in back of her instead, then made a beeline for the stairs to the second floor, to her room, where she locked herself in.

She leaned her head against the door, struggling to catch her breath. Nate was going to be here for another month. The situation was already untenable. What was she supposed to do now?

Obviously, the kiss in her office had been an error in judgment. So what had they done within five minutes of seeing each other again? Kissed. Awesome.

But that wasn't the real issue anyway.

He was here for a short while. He would be gone soon for a very long time. The way she liked him wasn't appropriate for a short-term fling. That was the core of the problem, and it wasn't negotiable. Feelings weren't.

Why she had to care this much about this man, she had no idea. There was no vote, no thoughts with pros and cons and doubts. Boom, she'd been punched in the heart and the head. If there had been a choice, she'd have nipped this business in the bud. But he'd kissed her, and she'd kissed him back. Twice. It was unrealistic to think things would get easier.

She pushed off from the door and took off her coat. She was still wearing her work clothes—black wool trousers, black blazer and a deep blueberry silk blouse. It was one of her favorite outfits, which she saved for special meetings or events. She'd had none of those things today.

All week she'd been dressing to impress him, on the off chance that she would see him, or more accurately, that he'd see her. Idiotic female behavior. As was the extra care she'd taken with her makeup, the time she'd spent last night over her pedicure, the gloss she'd put on her hair.

There had to be something she could do. Leaving wasn't an option. She hadn't heard the final word from Carnation yet, but she had a feeling she was going to have to start smaller if she wanted to compete in the label game. But she had gotten one new client. A small chain of automotive parts suppliers wanted Fitzgerald & Sons to do their catalogs. It was a good account, and their financial stability was rock-solid. It wasn't a game changer, though.

So that meant that Nate needed to be the one to leave.

She couldn't ask him to go back to Bali. But she could help him find a town house, then make sure he moved there for the duration of his stay.

How? She had no idea. She really didn't have time to go house hunting, let alone decorate a two-bedroom place for sublet. But this was an emergency, and she'd have to make time.

First thing? A call chain. She had five women she could always count on to phone at least five other women each when there was something that had to be done yesterday. She could get a few of them to take over the Easter basket duties. God, her mom could gather up a crowd in no time for that. So Shannon wouldn't supervise every last bit of candy placement. No one ever noticed the details anyway. More importantly, she'd put out the word for condos, town houses, duplexes, brownstones, whatever.

What was the use of doing favors for half the people from Little Italy to Midtown if she couldn't tap them for real-estate tips?

She'd include Nate's Realtor, get her excited. But before that she had to find out if Nate had made a decision on the condo they'd already seen. She doubted it. He would have said something.

Shannon changed into jeans and a sweater, then went downstairs for dinner. After that, the plan would go into motion, and she'd feel a hundred times better knowing she was taking action instead of simply sitting back, letting her hormones run her life.

She might not have a choice about who she fell for, but she was completely in charge of what she did once the die was cast.

"Has anybody done anything about it?" Nate asked.

Shannon hadn't rounded the corner to the dining

room yet, so she had no idea what Nate was talking about or to whom. That didn't seem to matter to her libido. His voice alone was enough to stir things that had no business being stirred as she was about to sit down for the family meal.

"What's there to do?"

It was Danny's voice, and Shannon hadn't realized he was coming by. That probably meant he expected to go prowling with Nate. So why was she disappointed? Problem solved. She wouldn't have to make an excuse about not doing something with him.

"It's private property, and they don't have the money to fix the court. They don't want to sell, either."

"Then the community should pay for it."

"Pay for what?" Shannon joined Nate, Danny and her father, who were all seated at the table.

"The basketball court." Nate frowned. "You saw what a mess it is. No wonder there were no kids playing. Somebody's got to be interested in fixing it up."

"What about your company?" she asked, looking at Nate as she tried to act as if everything was completely normal. "Brenner & Gill must do playgrounds and things when they build apartment complexes."

Nate stared at her for longer than would be acceptable in mixed company, but it wasn't her aura of glamour keeping him riveted. His eyes weren't even focused. He was thinking. When he snapped out of it, he shook his head. "It's not my company. Not mine alone, and there's no way Albert's going to want to donate our services, much less spring for materials and labor when he's on his way out. He never would have gone for it even when the company was rolling in contracts."

"He doesn't believe in contributing to the community?"

"No, nothing like that. He donates, but he's careful about where and how much, and what the company gets in return."

"That's a shame," she said. "I know how much that court meant to you two growing up."

Shannon's mom poked her head out from the kitchen. "If you think I'm waiting on you like this is the bloody Ritz, you've got another think coming."

Nate grinned, and Shannon returned it as Brady walked in to join them. "Head right to the kitchen, Brady," Nate said. "Your ma's on a tear."

Everyone pitched in to bring the big meal to the table, and Mr. Fitz did the carving of the corned beef. The beers came out, but Shannon passed, having water instead. The boys got to talking about fantasy leagues, and the food was delicious as always. Shannon watched as she ate, listened to how Nate spoke differently to Danny than he did to Brady. He was respectful, always, to her parents, but he had learned where he could tease and what he should ignore, and that compliments to Ma were always a good idea.

He was part of this family, there was no getting around it. He had listened to fights, gotten into fights, interrupted fights. He'd wept, he'd laughed and he'd bled at this very table.

But he wasn't her brother. He wasn't even the kid she'd grown up with. What he *was* made all her scattered wants and needs and likes and dislikes fall into place. He was the man she'd been looking for.

Who was only passing through.

9

NATE COULDN'T BELIEVE HOW many prime two-bedroom homes his Realtor had lined up for him. Or that Shannon had been free to come along for the viewings. That took some of the sting out of being hijacked by Danny last night. But she was here now and it was a good thing Aiko was completely professional and easygoing, because Shannon was not just on her game, but on fire.

Her eye for detail impressed him, but not as much as her practical sensibilities. She hadn't been swayed by inconsequential trappings, not at any of the five properties they'd been to this morning, and she was also quick to find the bottom line.

He couldn't help but imagine what she'd be like in a crisis. She was such a natural leader, she'd calm people instantly and she'd make practical decisions that would save lives. That was an incredible gift, one he hadn't really understood she possessed until today.

She'd be an asset anywhere. Now he got how that monstrous old printing plant was still in business, despite the antiquated equipment. Shannon wouldn't have it any other way. They'd have to move into digital printing soon. Or get a whole lot of new clients.

It wasn't a kind thought, not considering his loyalty to the family at large, but she was wasted at the plant. On the other hand, what did he know? He'd never had a family that valued loyalty or togetherness. Since he'd been in the States, he'd spoken to his sister twice and met her for a quick lunch. He liked his sister, he did, but they weren't connected the way Shannon and her brothers were.

She tugged on his sleeve. "You coming?"

"Yeah," he said. "Where are we going?"

"Are we boring you with finding your new home?"

He grabbed her hand and brought it to his lips for a kiss. "You're distracting," he said. "It's hard to look at storage space and dishwashers when you're so much more captivating."

She rewarded him with a blush, but she pulled her hand away. That was a shame because he hadn't lied. Touching Shannon in any capacity was his new obsession, and he wasn't a man known for getting carried away.

All his rules seemed to crumble in her wake. He'd been determined not to kiss her, yet he fully intended to do it again at the next opportunity. He knew that taking her to bed was an enormously stupid thing to do, and if he hadn't believed she'd regret it, he'd have gone after that, too.

He'd built his life around not being beholden to anyone. He was fond of his family, but he'd never made an adult decision about his life that took their wishes into consideration. Many people didn't understand that, especially not someone like Shannon, but that's who he was. Who he would continue to be.

"Well, come on," Shannon said, standing by a door that led…somewhere. He dutifully followed her, noticing how her slacks hugged her body, want for her riding low and hot in his body.

Ah, the master bedroom. Which was really big and nice. He was instantly drawn to the motorized blackout drapes.

"Just a toy," Shannon said. "You can write them in but don't let that influence you."

"A good toy, though," he said. "The bed's probably got a mattress that doesn't try to swallow me every night."

"I told you to switch rooms."

He almost said exactly where he'd prefer to sleep.

"The management company here charges a slightly higher fee than most," Aiko said, "but they have a sterling reputation. They screen everyone who works for them. Drug test, checkup on past employers. They're worth it."

"I like the layout," Shannon said, opening the closet door. It was huge for New York. You could actually walk inside the thing, although you couldn't walk far.

"If the bathrooms are as well-done as the kitchen, this place is a real contender." She walked into the bath, and he could tell by her sigh that it had passed the test.

He joined her at the door and nodded when he saw where she was staring. "Whirlpool bath."

"Look at the shower," she said. Then she walked into the glass-enclosed stall and turned on the water.

"What are you doing?"

"Checking the pressure. We're twelve floors up."

"You'll get soaked."

Undaunted, she rolled up the sleeve of her white blouse and stuck her hand under the stream. "Oh, yeah. I like this one."

"Aiko, are they getting action?"

"It only went on the market this morning. I was told we'd be the first to see it. I'm still not sure how she found out about it."

"She?"

Aiko nodded at Shannon.

Nate was puzzled. "You found it?"

"I told you at the wedding I'd ask around."

"Huh," he said. "That doesn't happen very often. I thought it was like 'Have a nice day' or 'Welcome to Walmart.'"

Shannon laughed, drying her hand with one of the guest towels. The town house had been staged for sale, which was smart. It was easier for him to get a feel for the place with furniture in situ. In fact… "Can we see about buying it as is? I like the way it's decorated."

"I can ask," Aiko said.

"Also," Shannon said, stepping closer to the pedestal sink, "can you see if they're amenable to a fast escrow?"

Aiko looked at the sheet she'd picked up from the seller earlier that morning. "Nate's prequalified, so I don't think they'll object. But it all depends on what kind of offer you want to make."

"Why don't we adjourn for lunch," Nate suggested. "We can discuss offers over food."

Both women nodded, and he escorted them out of the building. He would make sure to sit across from Aiko at lunch so he could focus on the business at hand. He wanted it over with so he could make plans with Shannon about the night ahead.

SHANNON SLIPPED OFF HER shoes and curled her toes into her bedroom rug. Today had gone more smoothly than she'd ever expected, which worried the hell out of her. The Easter baskets had been finished, all hundred of them, by her mother's book group. Shannon had thought it was hysterical when she'd heard the books they discussed were cookbooks, but then she'd been invited to a meeting and the lunch had been outrageously good. Her mom hadn't let her forget it.

Nate's offer had been submitted on that fantastic Bleeker Court co-op apartment. Her phone tree had come through in spades, and she owed Bree Kingston for that tip. Or maybe it was Bree's boyfriend, Charlie, who'd gotten the inside scoop.

Shannon opened her purse and took out Nate's trading card. She'd gotten it back from Ariel, who had been very disappointed. The pain hadn't run too deep, though, seeing as how she'd talked nonstop about her lawyer friend David during lunch. They hadn't gone out yet, but they had been meeting up after work for drinks. Other lawyers were there as well so it wasn't too suspicious. Shannon gave it two weeks at the most before they broke down and did the deed. They were only human, and Ariel was clearly over the moon about this guy.

Shannon knew what that felt like. But at least David and Ariel lived in the same country.

It didn't seem very fair that she'd finally found her perfect trading card man and she couldn't have him. A cosmic joke on her, she supposed. She'd put her heart and soul into the trading cards, not to mention her skills, and while she was happy for everyone who had met their match, she felt cheated.

After Nate went back to Indonesia, she'd start dating again. Maybe now that she knew what she wanted she'd be able to find someone like Nate. Probably not as funny, though. Or as sweet.

She put the card away, then changed into her favorite pair of worn jeans and a cozy sweater she'd had for ages. Her folks were out for the evening at a play. Her father had grumbled, but every once in a while he just had to suck it up and take his wife someplace nice to eat before a Broadway show.

Brady was staying at his girlfriend Paula's, as usual, and Danny had a work function so she knew he wouldn't be popping in unexpectedly. Which left her and Nate alone for the evening. He'd wanted to take her out, to thank her for the day, but she was tired, and she hadn't had a night to chill in a long while. They were going to order in Chinese food, then watch a movie.

It sounded great, but she wasn't at all sure if she'd be better off locking herself in her bedroom right now. Being alone with Nate was a huge risk. She wanted to believe she wasn't going to give in to her baser urges. After all, they were both adults. Responsible adults.

On the other hand, they probably wouldn't be alone again before Nate had to leave the country, and who knew when or if the sale would go through, so maybe one time wouldn't be all that terrible?

Oh. Damn.

NATE WASN'T USED TO THE house being so quiet. So empty. It had been the worst idea ever to stay in.

Now that they'd finished their dinner and were running through the pay-per-view movies, all he could think of was curling Shannon into his arms on the couch and making out like a couple of teenagers. As usual, his cock wasn't looking at the bigger picture, but for tonight making out would be fantastic. Dangerous beyond words. Still, fantastic.

"I don't want to see anything depressing," Shannon said, from all the way at the other end of the couch.

"Definitely not. Hate depressing."

She had her gaze on the LED TV above the fireplace, and her hand on the remote, clicking and clicking. She had socks on. Multicolored fuzzy socks. Under jeans that had been designed specifically to make her bottom look like the most gorgeous thing he'd ever seen. The sweater, however, was just mean. It was probably warm as all get-out, but it hid way too much. He could picture what was underneath, yes, but that wasn't a good idea. His imagination was already going crazy without trying to guess the exact pink of her nipples.

He bit back a groan and shifted on his section of the couch, stealthily adjusting his jeans. "Sure you don't want to take a walk over to Molly's?"

"It's karaoke night." The look she gave him expressed her feelings about amateur vocalists quite succinctly.

"We could sit far away from the speakers."

"We are sitting far away from the speakers."

She had a point. His point kept pressing harder against his fly. "All right, how about we go to Café Lalo and get some dessert? I've heard they have over a hundred kinds of cakes. Jazz, too. Coffee and chocolate cake, huh? Yeah?"

"Oh, God, after eating all that lo mein? I'd burst."

There had to be something in Manhattan that would convince Shannon to get up and go out, because he couldn't take this much longer. Sitting close, but not close enough. The memory of their kiss was the elephant in the room. A very large, very insistent elephant.

"This is supposed to be funny," she said.

He looked up at the TV. He'd seen the movie, hadn't liked it. "Saw it." Was she really that indifferent to their last kiss that she could flip through channels as if any movie on there was more interesting than the fact that the two of them were alone in the house? Frankly, it was kind of pissing him off.

"Okay, then you choose," she said, as she kept on clicking. Each time she paused, Nate said, "Saw it."

When she cleared her throat, he looked up from where he'd been staring at the area of her breasts beneath the Evil Sweater of Shattered Dreams. He smiled as benignly as he could.

"So Bali has a ton of multiplexes? Because I thought you said you didn't have a TV so you couldn't have cable or satellite, right?"

He nodded. "Tons of multiplexes. Practically on every street corner."

"For a man who travels the world and has seen countless amazing and wonderful things, you're a ridiculously bad liar."

"What do my travels have to do with it?"

She turned off the TV. "You don't want to be here. With me. You don't want to be here alone with me."

He exhaled loudly. "No. I don't."

"Okay, then," she said as she put down the remote. "I'll just leave you here to spend the evening however you like."

"Fine," he said, but then she stood up. "Wait, wait. That's not why. I *want* to be with you. I do. Come on, you didn't think I meant I didn't want to be with you."

She grinned at him. "No. I understood exactly what you were implying." She continued to smile as she walked toward him. But the closer she got, the more uncertain she appeared. Still, she kept on coming. "We could sit here and make out until someone comes home," she said, and then she flicked her gorgeous hair back behind her shoulder.

His breathing was becoming problematic. "Okay. I can do that. I can do the hell out of that."

She stopped slightly out of his reach. "But that's it. Just kissing. Because doing more than that would be a huge mistake. A giant, horrifying mistake."

"Horrifying?"

"No, I didn't mean it that way. It wouldn't be horrifying at all. Never. I'm so sorry. It wouldn't even be a mistake. Certainly not a huge mistake, because you're great. You're really...really great."

He took her hand. "And you're amazing. Now stop talking so we can start kissing."

She nodded. "Excellent advice." Shannon sat down next to him and put her hand on his thigh. "Think we can do this without getting ourselves in trouble?"

Shit. He wasn't about to lie. Besides, they both knew the answer to that question.

"There could be consequences." Her voice was low and serious, but her hand had moved up his thigh. Not far enough up his thigh.

"Like going to your bedroom?" he asked. "Because no one else is home? And we have the house to ourselves? Alone?"

She grinned at him. "You must be smoother than this. It's impossible for you to have lived your incredible life and been this dorky with women. Look at the way you dress."

"You're not just any woman."

Her breath caught and he watched the beauty of her blush blossom across her pale, pale skin. He stared into eyes that had grown dark with want. He was hoping as hard as he'd ever hoped that she'd want to use that bed of hers right now. He had a condom...well, two condoms…in his wallet. And he wanted to take off her sweater more than he wanted to breathe.

"I'm pretty sure we're about to make that mistake we were talking about," she whispered as her hand moved one last inch.

HE LED HER UPSTAIRS, AND Shannon could hear his harsh breathing, but that wasn't caused by the climb. Neither was her own thundering heartbeat. They were going up to her room, and she was being stupid, stupid, so stupid that it broke records for being stupid. Not that she cared. Because she wanted him, and this might be it. Her one chance.

Honestly, it wasn't that much of a mistake. She was already going to go through hell when he left. At least now she'd have a sexy memory to keep her warm at night. Until she got over him, which she most definitely would.

They reached the second floor, and he walked so fast she was practically running to keep up with him. She liked that a lot. He pulled her inside her bedroom, then slammed the door so hard she jumped, and then he locked it. The next second she was in his arms and his mouth covered hers.

He slid his hands under her sweater and the first touch on her warm skin was electric. He moved quickly up to her bra and surprised her by passing right by her breasts.

"Off," he whispered against her lips. "Off now."

Ah. She stepped back and let him tug up the sweater and toss it away. Good thing she'd decided to wear one of her pretty bras and matching blue panties.

He stared, wide-eyed with wonder, as if he'd never seen such fabulous lingerie, which she knew couldn't be true. If he liked the undergarment so much, she wondered what he'd look like when she reached behind and undid the clasp.

She stretched out the moment, the performer in her loving the standing ovation in his pants. When she finally let the bra fall to the floor, his lips parted and he slowly blinked.

"Pink," he said.

"Pink?"

He nodded. "Perfect and pink. God."

She wouldn't have guessed she'd be this nervous, not with Nate, but the way he was staring at her…wow. With unsteady fingers she undid her jeans and let them drop, then toed off her socks.

He was unbuttoning his shirt so fast she thought he'd pop a button. She'd already seen his chest, but it was a welcome sight especially since she would get to touch it this time.

He ripped his wallet out of his pocket, took out two condoms and put them on the nightstand. Then he shook off his jeans the same way he danced. Adorably. Next it was shoes and socks, and he didn't even try to pretend that he wasn't hot and aching for her. When he stood up after slipping off his boxers, he was so hard his erection pressed against his stomach.

She swallowed thickly at the heat that filled her from the inside out. He was stunning, and, oh, the way he wanted her.

10

NATE TOOK HER HANDS AND pulled her back with him until he sat down on her bed. Her breasts were a most incredible sight, but not nearly enough.

He put his fingers underneath the edge of her panties and pushed them down, laying kisses on the soft, sweet, pale skin all the way down to the top of her red, red triangle. "Oh, God," he said as her panties dropped and he sat back, needing some distance to see the total picture and also to slow down. It would be a shame to hurry through this. "You're…"

"Thank you."

He looked up at her. "You are."

"So are you."

He reached behind her, his large hands on her waist, and he drew her closer. He breathed in the scent of her as he bent to that incredible patch of brilliant red hair and he kissed her right there before he moved down. He nuzzled against her until his lips found her soft folds.

She gasped above him, her fingers snaking through his hair.

"Spread your legs," he whispered.

Either the words or his breath did something for

her, if her shiver was anything to go by. She parted her thighs, and he moaned as he kissed her, savoring her taste as he explored with his tongue.

He wasn't able to reach everything, not in the position he was in, but that would be all right. He got far enough to make her squirm, to make her tug at his hair as he became more and more focused. God, she tasted so good, and his hands had moved down to her lush, round buttocks. He squeezed them none too gently. Her moan said she had no complaints.

He'd felt her tense. Her body had grown rigid, and dammit, he couldn't stand the angle so he pushed her back until he could drop to his knees.

Now it was both hands on his head, and she quivered in his arms. He had that little nub of hers held between his lips and he sucked hard before he used his tongue once more.

Shannon cried out above him. She pulsed her hips forward, pressing herself down on his tongue, and then she froze, just froze as he felt her body spasm in release.

He didn't stop until she made him. When he stood, they were both panting, and her cheeks were as pink as her nipples. He kissed her, threw back the sheets and finally got them both horizontal.

The feel of her trembling from knee to chest was a full body rush. His hand went to her shoulder, then down. At the first hint of the curve of her breast, he paused, rolled over to grab a condom and sheath himself. When he came back to her, it was with a heartfelt sigh. "I want more," he said. "I want everything."

"Yes," she whispered, her voice more breath than sound. She ran her palm down his chest, right to his nipple, which she proceeded to rub and tug between two of her fingers.

He moaned, and when he cupped her breast at last, she whispered, "Now, please."

He moved his legs between her thighs, took hold of himself and entered her. Nothing in his life had ever felt better than that slow slide.

SHANNON TREMBLED ONCE he was flush inside her. Her head fell back on the pillow as she groaned her pleasure. He was made for her body, exactly the right everything that made her feel wonderful and wicked.

She'd already known his kisses fit her to a T, but she hadn't known what his body would feel like as it rubbed against hers, and she hadn't imagined how his hands would thrill her.

He rolled his tongue over her beaded nipple and she arched her back, pushing her breast into his mouth.

He caught her legs and pulled them around his hips, then ran his hand up the bottom of her thigh. Pushing with his palm, he encouraged her to bring her knees closer to her chest.

Nate moved in tighter, deeper. "Look at me," he said, his voice as low as she'd ever heard it.

She hadn't realized she'd closed her eyes. Staring into his gaze while they were so incredibly connected exaggerated every sensation. Not just the flush that was the beginning of yet another orgasm, but how his hard chest rubbed against her nipples and his breath brushed across her lips. Shuddering, she reached up to touch his face but she had no strength in her arm and it fell back against the sheets. He bent his head and kissed her right knee, his gaze never wavering from hers.

With a small controlled thrust, he drove in deeper, rocking against her, so deep, the pressure so unbearable that she gasped and jerked. Instinctively she clenched her muscles, squeezing him, and he tensed.

"Oh, God, no, no, I can't be this close yet," he said, his expression tortured as he held himself completely still.

Wet and slippery with longing, she bucked, trying to get him to move again. He slipped his fingers between them, knowing exactly where and how to touch, and way sooner than she'd have ever guessed a second jolt of heat shot through her body and she spasmed around him, knocking his hand loose and letting out a startled cry.

He started to withdraw, but before she could object, he drove in deeper and after two thrusts he cried out her name as he stilled, as the muscles of his body tightened.

By the time her legs fell to the bed and he rolled to her side, she had relearned how to breathe. She looked at him, all sweaty and gorgeous, lying on her pillow. "That was…"

"Amazing," he said, his voice ragged. "Incredible."

Shannon grinned, feeling like she'd had too much to drink, or hadn't had enough oxygen or some other crazy thing that made the world spin faster. She found his hand by her thigh and she folded her fingers between his. "You have to be back in Bali when?"

"Not for a while."

"So you're not leaving tonight."

He smiled. "Nope. Why? You have something in mind for later?"

"It's possible." She smiled.

He brought their joined hands up to his lips so he could kiss her fingers. A different kind of pleasure shimmered through her.

She closed her eyes, letting her heartbeat slow as she rubbed her foot up his calf. He made contented sounds, and soon he was gently rubbing her from belly to chest. Sensual and slow, a perfect interlude.

When he moved, it was to kiss her tummy before he sat up. "Did I tell you how terrific you were at the property showings?"

She laughed. It was unexpected, but then he'd surprised her at every turn. "No, you didn't."

"I'm serious. You should run for office or something. You'd straighten this city out in six months. They wouldn't know what to do with someone as clever as you."

She looked up at him to find him looking back. He was completely serious. "Stop. I've already got too much of an ego."

"I think you're wonderful and I'm not about to stop saying so."

"Well, thanks."

He squeezed her hand before he let it go. "I'm going to make a run to the bathroom, then I'm going to get my robe, then I'm coming back here to ravish you again. But first—" he stood and pulled the comforter and sheet up across her chest "—I'm going to kiss you."

It felt odd and sexy when he bent over her to capture her lips, him being naked when she was covered up. When that ended, which wasn't for several long, delicious minutes, he disappeared out her door, and she stretched like a cat under the sheet. She closed her eyes and pushed her fingers through her hair and it was very quiet. No footsteps from the floor above, no music from Brady's room. Just the sound of her breathing.

Her brain, the one that had convinced her that this was the best idea ever, was starting to back down a bit, and the voice of real life was becoming more than a whisper. She'd known—how could she not have known?—that everything she'd felt about Nate before would be nothing compared to what she felt now. She wasn't sorry. Given a chance to do it again, she would. But she'd better prepare herself for a hell of a blow when he left. It was going to take some serious time to get over him. She hadn't considered the memory of his skin, of how they fit together, of what he looked like when his eyes were dark with want and, God, how he said her name.

Yeah. It was gonna be a bitch. Because while she had no doubt how very much he wanted her, she also knew he didn't want her for very long.

NATE SLIPPED ON HIS BATHROBE as quietly as he could, not wanting to wake Shannon. The light was on beside the bed, but that hadn't stopped her from falling asleep. He wished he could succumb himself, but he had to get back to Myles's room. It wasn't likely that anyone would come knocking, but he wasn't going to take the risk.

Leaving should have been easy. So much about Shannon was. Conversation, laughter, touching. He'd never had sex with someone who'd been a longtime friend before, and now he saw the appeal, although they hadn't actually been friends. She'd been a presence in his life, and he in hers, the only thing they'd had in common was the rest of the family. In all the years he'd come to her home, they'd never sat down and had a private conversation.

They had grown accustomed to each other, nonetheless. Since first seeing her in her green bridesmaid's dress, he'd felt drawn to her. He'd never have imagined he would know what she looked like when she came undone. That giving her pleasure would be right up there in the sexiest things he'd ever experienced

"What are you doing?" Shannon hadn't opened her eyes and her voice was mumbles and exhaustion.

"Go back to sleep."

"Don't leave. It's the middle of the night."

He leaned over and brushed some hair away from her cheek. "I know. That's why I'm leaving."

She sniffed and rubbed her head into her pillow, shaking loose the silky hairs he'd pushed back. "Don't leave," she said again.

Was he going to break every rule? There was no reason to think anyone would come looking for either of them on a Sunday morning, but the chance existed. He kissed her gently, then whispered, "Sleep well."

Shannon didn't stir.

Nate went back to the bed from hell and tried to get comfortable. The sheets were cold, the mattress continued to suck, and instead of his usual après-sex relief at being alone, he felt…something else. He could imagine so clearly what it would have been like to curl up in back of Shannon, tuck in his knees, circle her waist and breathe her in as he drifted to sleep.

It would have been nice to watch her wake up. He had this image in his head that she was one of those people who went from sleep directly to alert. When he'd run into her after his shower, she'd had none of the somnambulist haze about her.

But he couldn't be sure. She could wake up drowsy and tousled and blinking, and Christ, how was his cock even thinking of getting hard? They'd wrung each other out. He'd come twice, while she'd come at least three times, maybe more. He wasn't good enough at reading her yet to be sure.

Now, there was a project worth tackling. He'd begun, but only in the most fundamental ways. Her nipples were moderately sensitive, which was rare, but the little spot behind her ear drove her crazy. She had a thing for being somewhat constricted. Twice, he'd held her wrists up above her head as he'd done wicked things to her body, and it was like plugging her into a socket.

He'd loved how responsive she'd been when he'd hunkered down between her thighs. God, she'd smelled incredible. His head still ached from where she'd tugged his hair a little too enthusiastically. Not that he'd minded.

But there was still much to learn. More to taste, to touch, to try. Problem was, how…and when? Far more problematically, where? She was incredibly busy with work and her side projects. He'd been astonished that she'd come out with him to look at the properties, and it wasn't likely they'd have another night where they'd be alone in the house.

He should hear quickly about the offer on the co-op. Since the owners were out of the city Aiko had given them forty-eight hours to respond. He'd offered just under the asking price, so he figured he had a good shot. The furniture was already out, so he hoped they'd be willing to close quickly. And if not, he simply had to move back into the hotel. Yeah, he liked staying here with the Fitzes, but it was pretty clear that it had become more about staying close to Shannon.

IT WAS LATE MORNING BY THE time she awoke. Still, she wasn't anxious to hop out of bed right away. Nate's scent was all over the pillows and the sheets, and she lazily rolled over, her body aching but in a good way. She buried her face in his pillow and inhaled deeply, the memory of him inside her still so vivid a frisson of excitement raced through her.

She'd stay there for an hour if she could, reliving every moment, basking in satisfaction, but she had to go to work for a few hours. There was payroll to do, and signs to be printed up for the Easter egg hunt. Then she needed to look over the baskets, check out the condition of the back room where her mother and friends had worked so hard.

Thinking of her mother propelled Shannon into her robe and into the bathroom. Best of all worlds, she would be gone by the time her parents returned from mass, but that was unlikely. Her mother would want to know what had kept Shannon up so late that she'd slept in. Mothers didn't care how old their daughters were when it came to Sundays. Her mother in particular would poke at Shannon until she coughed up some kind of excuse.

If asked for details, Shannon would deftly change the subject to the payroll, and that would be that. It was an underhanded thing to do, given her mother's guilt at leaving the accounting to Shannon, but all was fair in…

Not love or war. Just evasion, plain and simple.

It really was time for her to move out of the house. As much as she loved her family and this house, she yearned for the freedom. Yes, she would resent paying rent to live in a strange apartment, especially knowing how exorbitant rents were in the city, but last night had shown her how impossible it was that she still lived with her parents. It had nothing to do with Nate. She wasn't fooling herself in any way. He would leave at some point, she knew that.

She turned on the water in the shower, then stripped and stood under the spray. It was foolish to start worrying about moving out yet. There would be plenty of time for that when Nate was out of the country, out of her life. Then there would be the inevitable fall....

Okay, she was not going down that path. Nate wasn't gone. He was here right now. There would be time enough for regrets later. Today, she would be happy to see him. If she were lucky, they would be able to spend time together tonight. If not tonight, then soon.

She couldn't afford to let this fling take over her life. First came the job, the very important business of getting new clients. Everything else came in at a distant second, including her sex life.

If there was one thing she'd mastered, it was how to prioritize. As much as she liked Nate, he wasn't at the top of the list. Even if she wanted him to be.

11

DANNY SPRAWLED AGAINST the booth back at Molly's, his second beer nearly gone and his gaze meandering over a couple of girls who didn't look old enough to drive, let alone drink. Nate glanced at his watch, wondering when Shannon was going to get there. He hadn't seen her since yesterday morning except in passing. It hadn't been intentional, just bad timing. But he'd thought about her. Too often.

"Yeah, no, the work is good," Danny said. "I mean, it's decent for an ad firm. There's only gonna be so much freedom in an environment like Madison Avenue. But I'm starting to put together a portfolio of my own stuff, you know? On the internet."

"That must be easier than getting a gallery showing."

"Yeah, but it's easier for everyone else, too, so you still need to get the showings. Maybe now more than ever. I'm getting there, though. I've had a few private commissions."

"Yeah? Why haven't I seen any of your work?"

Danny grunted. "Because you're a selfish pig who never asked."

"Yeah, I love you, too, bro. Seriously, what's it under? Your name?"

"Yeah." Danny sat up straighter and pulled out what looked like a baseball card from his back pocket and flicked it over to Nate.

"This is yours?"

"No, I'm showing you my aunt Martha's artwork. Of course it's mine."

The picture on the cover of the trading card was striking as hell. Like some of the best graphic-novel work he'd seen, right up there with Alan Moore and Dave Gibbons. "You're kidding me with this, right?" he asked.

"What?"

Nate stared at him. "You're an illustrator? These commissions, have they been for comics?"

Danny smiled at him. "Not yet. I know I should have told you before now what I was doing, but I wanted to… Anyway, I'm getting my stuff out there. I've had a few calls, had a few encouraging rejections. In the meantime the day job is great, if a person has to have a day job."

"You were always drawing something, mostly where you weren't supposed to. But not stuff like this. You were into street art. Like Banksy or something." Nate grinned. "Remember that wall behind the supermarket?"

Danny nodded as he laughed. "I thought for sure we were going to jail."

"You and me both. How long were we stuck under that crate?"

"Three hours?"

"It felt like three years." Nate turned over the card. Read the short bio and the contact info, and admired the two other small images. "This is clever," he said, holding up the card. "You did this at your plant, huh?"

Danny nodded. "Lots of artists do trading cards. It's a thing now."

"Huh. Can I keep this?"

"What do you think?" Danny asked, then signaled Peggy the waitress. "The pisser is I'd be able to quit the day job and concentrate all my energy on illustration if it weren't for the Princess."

Nate put down the card. "What do you mean?"

Danny sighed. "She's determined to keep the old bucket of a printing plant running. Man, she kills herself over it and my folks won't let anyone tell her she's wasting her time."

"Wasting her time?"

"You have any idea how much money the folks are sitting on with that place? They want to retire. My father says Ireland, and Ma just laughs and gets secret brochures from Florida. Brady's been offered a couple of great jobs that he can't take because the Princess isn't supposed to know that trading cards aren't ever going to be enough, although to be fair, he wouldn't mind staying at the plant forever. But the truth is we're losing textbook contracts and catalogues. The land is worth so much more than the business, it's not even funny. The whole situation is the stupidest thing I've ever heard of. We're talking millions of dollars. That's not even counting selling off the equipment. And then if we sold the house? Shit."

"The business has been in your family for generations. And the house? No way your parents would let go of the house," Nate said, even though the thought had crossed his mind. Yeah, he'd said something about it to Shannon, but he hadn't been serious.

"Wanna bet?"

Nate took a drink of his Guinness as the new data sunk in. "And everyone knows this but Shannon?"

"The neighbors know, the mailman knows. Unfortunately, the employees aren't idiots and they're just waiting for the shoe to fall. They're upset especially since the benefits aren't what they used to be. Everyone's surly, and it's only a matter of time before someone manufactures an accident so they can sue. The plant is outdated, my old man won't upgrade 'cause he doesn't want to refinance and get stuck. It's a losing situation from every angle, all because no one wants to hurt Shannon's feelings."

"She'll be crushed."

"I know. We all know. It's gonna tear her up." Danny shook his head. "That's where you come in."

"What?"

Danny sat up, leaned over the table, his beer forgotten. "You and Shannon, you've been getting along really well. She likes you, and you're practically family. And you're good with hard stuff. I mean, you're used to helping people who've lost everything. Believe me, she's not going to lose anything. She'll walk away not having to worry about money to get herself situated, figure out what she wants to do."

"You want me to tell her?"

Danny stared at him. "Yeah. Not straight-out, not mean or anything. Maybe let her know you overheard Ma talking about Florida. About Brady's job offers. You're dealing with real estate right now—you could mention how much the land is worth."

Nate felt as if he'd been punched in the gut. He almost admitted that he'd already made a passing comment but that was before the other night. Before he and Shannon had… "For God's sake, Danny."

"It's a hell of a lot to ask. And we all know we're going to have to talk. As a family. But maybe you could just think about it, huh? You'd be good with her. You can kind of pave the way to the big showdown. We all need to move on, including her."

"Man. She's been fighting so hard for the family. For a legacy."

"You don't have to, buddy. We'll come up with another idea. I don't mean to get you caught up in our mess."

The waitress came by with a couple more drinks and Danny flirted with her a bit, his discomfort with the topic of conversation obvious. Nate couldn't give him an answer, not until he thought long and hard about what Danny wanted him to do. Particularly now.

"You all set, honey?"

Nate smiled at Peggy, but his heart wasn't in it. Shannon would be devastated. It was a damn shame, too, because she was incredibly talented and would be an asset anywhere. If he thought he had a chance, he'd try to get her to come work for The International Rescue Committee. But he wouldn't even try. Gramercy was woven into the fabric of her life and he'd never dream of taking her away. She should run for city council. She'd see to it that corner basketball courts weren't left to rot and ruin.

But that was the long view. In the short term, discovering her family wanted a separate future more than they cared about their collective past was going to cripple her.

"Speak of the devil," Danny said, leaning back in his seat again. "The Princess hath arrived."

"Don't call her that anymore. She doesn't like it." A wave of anger at his friend made his gut tense. It wasn't logical. Danny was right. She was tilting at windmills. The business had been going downhill for a long time, but he hated like hell that he'd been asked to be the messenger.

She came up to the table and smiled at Nate in a way that made him want to whisk her to Bali and help her forget all about New York and family ties. "Shove over," she said. "I'm tired, thirsty and I have really exciting news. But first, did you hear back from Aiko?"

"Not yet." Nate moved, but not much. He wanted to be able to touch her. "What's so exciting?"

"Who's Aiko?" Danny asked. "You holding out on me?"

"The Realtor" was all Nate said. He'd already told Danny about the back-and-forth countering that was driving Nate nuts. Right now he wanted to know about Shannon.

She gave him a dazzling smile, then turned to search out the waitress. "Give me a minute." She put her purse on the outside of the booth, then let her head drop forward. Her hair cascaded into a fiery pool on the tabletop, until she sat up straight again when Peggy came to take their order.

"I'll have the chicken Caesar salad, dressing on the side."

"Screw that," Danny said. "I want the potpie, but first I want the calamari."

Nate wasn't very hungry anymore, but he still said, "I'll have the grilled salmon, please."

"'Please'?" Peggy said, sounding confused. "What's that word mean again?" Then she looked at Shannon. "Your regular?"

Shannon frowned. "Water, thanks."

Danny's brows went up. "What's with all the dressing-on-the-side business? You hate that."

"I have to look my best," she said, then grinned like she'd just won Miss Congeniality. "Because the camera adds ten pounds."

"TV?" Nate smiled back at her, even knowing what he knew. She looked so damn happy. "They're doing a reality show about your life?"

She waved him away as if he'd been joking, but now that he thought about it, she'd be great at that. "I'm being interviewed by WNYC. About Easter at the park. They've asked me to come in on Thursday. It'll be live, on *Local Happenings with Grant and Lisa*."

Nate took her hand and squeezed it. "That's terrific. What's the station?"

"It's not a big affiliate or anything," she said. "A local independent that broadcasts in Manhattan and some parts of New Jersey. But everyone watches it. They talk about what's going on in town, and sometimes they do exposés on petty local scandals and profile pieces on charities and people who are making a difference. But mostly they announce book fairs and library programs, stuff like that."

"The Easter thing is where you raise money for the church renovations?" Danny asked.

"Nope. That's our Christmas program. This benefits outreach programs for feeding the homeless. But in each of the gift baskets there are cards from Fitzgerald and Sons, and we're handing out trading cards to everyone who comes to the park. Two of the food trucks are letting me put up big banners. You know I'm going to talk about the printing plant when I'm interviewed."

"There's not a doubt in my mind," her brother said, then shot a glance at Nate.

Shannon glowed as she went on about her plans, and as she talked, Nate thought about what Danny had asked him to do. An interview about Easter baskets wasn't going to save the day. In fact, it made things worse. Getting her hopes up. Putting that look in her eyes.

He didn't want to think about it, but after the interview was over, someone was going to have to tell her that the rest of the family wasn't on board with her plans.

It made horrible sense that it should be him. He owed the Fitzgeralds so much, and he couldn't picture any of them breaking the news to her. Theoretically he was part of the family, for good and bad, and this was not going to be good. But he would be careful. As careful as he'd ever been in his life. He'd try and take as much of the sting away as possible.

And he sure wasn't going to bring it up before she had her last hurrah.

"You're tired," he said, his voice low, close to her ear.

"I am," she agreed, letting her thumb run over the back of his hand as they walked slowly in the direction of home. She should probably be concerned about someone spotting them, but she wasn't. "It's a good tired."

"Probably don't want some crazy man sneaking into your boudoir later."

"Depends," she said, smiling in the dark. "How much later?"

"Fifteen minutes?"

She laughed. "Is that starting now, or when we cross the threshold?"

"Fine. We'll wait. The basketball game's over, though.

It's past your mother's bedtime. So it's only your dad, right? Or will Brady be home?"

"No, he's not there, and Dad likes to be in bed for the eleven o'clock news."

"There you go. So, fifteen minutes after the start of the news."

"Fine. Jeez. So impatient."

He pulled her to a stop between streetlamps. "Damn right I'm impatient. I've never slept with a TV star before."

"Well, whoever she is, you can tell her to get in line. I've got you booked for the night."

He pulled her in as if they'd been dancing, her coat billowing behind her as she stepped into his arms. His kiss made an excellent day perfect. He tasted of beer, while she, being the most considerate person ever, tasted like peppermint. But she wasn't complaining. Every kiss she got from Nate was another memory she'd store away.

There was another one, a quick brush of lips, but still sweet, three doors down, and then she was at the big red door, her key at the ready. Nate's hand touched hers, stilling the turn. "I forgot something," he said. "I'll be back in half an hour."

"What?"

"Condoms. I meant to—"

"Top shelf, medicine cabinet. Big old box. Probably Brady's but he shouldn't miss them. Grab a handful."

Nate's eyes opened very wide.

"Not all for tonight. For God's sake, I've got work in the morning."

He laughed and followed her inside, where the downstairs was quiet, and the evening was about to get juicy. After hanging up their coats, they hurried to the second floor. Luckily, Brady's room was dark just like the rest of the hall. As if it were some kind of spy mission, Nate gave her a nod before he peeled off to Myles's room. She hurried to her own and got undressed as quickly as she could.

Her thoughts were tripping over themselves, first about Nate, then about the interview, then back to Nate. She made a quick trip to the bathroom, and when she closed the bedroom door behind her, she let all her thoughts of Easter eggs and interviews go in favor of picturing how she wanted to look when Nate came in.

Robe off or on? Her first thought was off, but naked on the bed seemed so normal. Although he really liked her hair. Maybe she could arrange it so that it covered certain bits....

Nate wouldn't care at all. It wasn't a show, and she wasn't trying to dazzle him. He liked her. She liked him. They were good together. For now.

Her robe slid off her shoulders, and she pushed the comforter back on the bed. He would be here in a moment, and her heart was already beating faster, her nipples getting hard. He'd been so happy for her. Cheering her on.

The line she straddled was thin. Too much optimism and she feared the eventual crash would smash her beyond help. Too much pragmatism and why bother?

Two quick taps came seconds before he slipped inside and locked the door. It still felt like a spy novel, and that was good. The element of drama was important in this fragile game.

"You take my breath," he said, walking slowly toward her. He was James Bond sexy in his robe. All he was missing was the martini. It helped that he'd run his hand through his hair, that his eyes were already dark with arousal.

"I'll give it back before you leave." She reached for his belt, then pushed the robe off, and the press of his skin on hers made everything fuzzy. He kissed her long and slow as they maneuvered between the sheets, breaking only when absolutely necessary. Finally, though, their heads were on pillows and his knee was between her thighs.

"I almost came here last night."

"Why didn't you?" She smiled at the feathery swirls he idly traced on her belly.

"I had a very long conversation with myself. I was completely unreasonable for the most part." He pressed a warm, moist kiss to the side of her jaw, then trailed his lips to her ear. "God, I can be an idiot."

Her eyes briefly drifted closed. "How so?"

"I'd almost convinced myself that it would be in both our best interests for me to wake you at one-thirty in the morning when you had to be up at six o'clock."

"That's not idiotic."

He lifted his head, moving the breath that had been warming the back of her ear to her cheek. "I ended up being noble. What did I get wrong?"

"It would have been okay, that's all. If you'd come."

"It was one-thirty."

"I know. I'd have let you in." She slid her palm across the contours of his chest. He felt so damn good. So solid and safe. So Nate. "Turns out I like you."

He kissed her, smiling. She felt his grin, then matched it with her own. When he pulled back, his gaze grew serious and the smile faded. "I wish you didn't have to go to work tomorrow. You could reacquaint me with your city."

"You lived here most of your life."

A single finger trailed down her neck, then lower, all the way to her breast. "That's true, but I never lived in your city. Mine was crowded and noisy and selfish. You love yours so much it has to be something special."

It was an odd thing for him to say, even his voice sounded a bit strained. She searched his face, but if something was wrong, his expression gave nothing away. "It's New York," she said. "Of course it's special. It's the best city in the world."

One hand was holding up his head, while the other continued to play with her body. It felt delicious and intimate for all its unconsciousness, so she settled down and dismissed her initial reaction as her own weirdness.

He'd switched from the single digit to all the fingers and sometimes the palm as he traced her, mapped her. Everywhere he went left a trail of sparks, and it was difficult to split her attention between the sensation and his words. But she wanted both. It was important to fit in everything she could while she had the chance.

"How many big cities have you been to?" he asked. "Paris? Florence? Sydney?"

She shook her head, shifting to her side a little more so she could get in on the touching action. She ran her hand up his hip and kept on going. "The only foreign city I've been to is Toronto. Which was wonderful, but it wasn't New York."

"Too bad you haven't visited Europe. It's not a bad plane ride from here."

"Nope. When I was young, my parents were always at the plant. Now I'm always at the plant. It's the curse of a family-run business."

"That's crazy."

"That's real life."

"Well, see," he murmured, "now the best is yet to come." He kissed her nose, then her lips, and that was the end of talking. That hand of his got serious. When he slipped between her thighs, stroking lightly on the tender flesh, she tipped onto her back, thrusting up with her hips to show him she wanted more.

Two fingers pushed inside her and before she could grab hold of any part of him, he was down the bed. He licked her all over and around where his fingers were before he settled in with pointed tongue.

Her knees went up and her heels dug into the mattress as he kept thrusting inside her, kept circling her clit with ever increasing pressure and speed.

Shannon's back arched with exquisite tension, her hands fisted the sheets, and she could already feel the beginning of her orgasm starting low and deep.

"Now," she said. She lifted her head and tried to focus. "Now, please, Nate, now."

He looked at her from where he sucked her nub between his lips, and she could see he didn't want to stop, but she did. As wonderful as it was, she wanted him inside her.

"Please."

He let her go, his fingers as reluctant as his mouth.

She had enough sanity left to grab one of the condoms on the night table, but he had to take it from there. Even though he wasn't touching her, except for his knees against her inner thighs, she was still close, still trembling, still moving her body as if his cock were already buried to the base.

Seconds later, he was there, he was sliding in and groaning as if it were the best feeling he'd ever had in his life.

The way he filled her made her writhe, made her

crazy, and when she tasted herself on his tongue as he kissed her, she made noises she'd never heard before.

She came from his thrusting. He didn't use his fingers again, and neither did she. But she came and the sensation was so strong she nearly bucked him off.

"Jesus, Shannon," he said, holding her hips as if he'd never let her go. "I can't…"

He came while she was still shuddering with aftershocks. There wasn't enough air in the world to fill her lungs, and her heart was beating itself out of her chest, and oh, God, it was unbelievable.

"I've never…" she said between deep gasps. "I've never had that happen before."

Nate had pulled out, flopped next to her. "What?"

"I've never come from intercourse alone."

He looked at her and grinned. Smugly. "No kidding."

"It's true. You do have mad skills."

"I'm inspired. You're amazing. Everything about you gives me such pleasure."

She curled into his side and brushed her hand across his chest. "I know. You, too."

He petted her arm for a while. "Where would you go?" he asked. "If you could go anywhere at all?"

"Um, I'm not sure. Paris. London. I've always wanted to go there. Rome, Florence, Switzerland, India, a safari in Africa, Machu Picchu, the Netherlands, Australia, New Zealand, Banff—"

His laughter made her head bounce on his chest.

"What?"

"You surprise me. I was starting to think you'd evolved into a typical stagnant New Yorker."

"Hey."

"Don't get me wrong. That's a lot of dreams and I'm glad you have them," he said.

She sniffed. "That's all they are. Dreams."

"Don't say that."

"It's true, but it's not as if I'm trapped in some urban tragedy. It's my family we're talking about. Everything we've built for generations. I'm doing my part, is all. Times are tough, but the plant will—"

He squeezed her arm. "I don't want to talk about the plant. In fact, I want you to pretend that you don't have anything standing in your way. You've got the time, the money, the freedom to go wherever you want. Where would you go first?"

"No responsibilities, huh?"

"Exactly."

"I don't think my imagination is that good."

"Sure it is. It's just pretend. You can go anywhere on earth. Where would it be? The first place?"

She sighed and let the reality float away, let herself imagine a life that couldn't be. "An island, I think," she said. "Somewhere exotic and quiet and mystical."

"Ah, now you're talking my language." He brushed her skin with the tips of his fingers. "That's Bali. It's a magical place. The mountains, the caves. The people are so generous, and you can lose yourself in the green jungles or in the water with coral reefs and brilliant fish all around you. Take a whole day and wander the beaches, or go to the temple where the monkeys are sacred. The scent of incense mixed with the smells of the earth, the water, the sky. It's so beautiful there, Shannon, I don't have enough words. It's paradise."

Shannon's eyes were closed and she tried to picture herself on his island, but the passion he had for his true home overshadowed his descriptions. "It sounds perfect."

"It is."

She smiled and kissed his chest. Promised herself she'd be brave and not choke on the words. "And you can't wait to get back there."

He stilled beneath her. Not even breathing.

12

NATE PURPOSELY LEFT FOR his noon lunch at ten. The meeting was at Eleven Madison Park, in the Flatiron District, and he wanted to walk. It was a beautiful day, he hadn't even worn a coat, just his suit jacket. He headed north on 3rd Avenue, thinking about everything that had happened since his conversation with Danny at the pub.

There were a lot of things he'd had to do in his life that were unpleasant, even painful. He'd witnessed the devastation caused by tsunamis and earthquakes on people's lives and their communities. But he'd been there to help people recover and rebuild. Now he was being asked to rip apart the foundations of Shannon's life, and it was burning a hole in his gut.

All that travel talk had been illuminating. He'd wanted to get a feel for how much of her dedication was something she chose versus something she hadn't been able to avoid. Naturally, he'd hoped her choices had been limited, and that letting the plant go would be liberating, but that wasn't what he'd heard. Yes, it was hard and she'd sacrificed a lot, but she hadn't been forced. At least not on a conscious level.

He'd wondered when he saw that big sign outside Fitzgerald & Sons how Shannon had felt about being overlooked. She'd been a surprise to the family, five years after they'd stopped trying for a girl, but still, she must have felt like an outsider from time to time. She wasn't one of the boys in other ways, as well. She'd been a show pony to their workhorses. That they still called her Princess said so much.

Finding out the truth wouldn't kill her, but it would be a close thing. At least for a while. Her emotional investment was so complete he doubted she gave herself any room to imagine a different kind of life. She'd have to start from the ground up. It wouldn't be a quick transition, that's for sure.

So basically, he was going to yank the rug right out from under her, then disappear, leaving her to find her way alone.

That sucked. That sucked so hard he wanted to smash something. He slowed his pace, surprised that he'd been speed walking. Escaping? He was on Lexington, at East 26th, at the Armory in Kips Bay, and he had barely any recollection of how he'd gotten there. The building was a beautiful example of Beaux-Arts architecture, one of his personal favorites. But then a lot of buildings in the city were his favorites.

The Flatiron. The neo-Gothic New York Life Insurance Company, the marble courthouse on East 25th. Hell, the fantastic houses all around Gramercy Park were where he'd head when he needed to be on his own. Somehow, he'd always end up in one of the small green corners that weren't exactly private, but not precisely parks. Or the basketball courts. There'd been so many when he was a kid, and had he passed a single one on his way up here?

He might have been walking in a daze, but he'd have stopped if there'd been an inviting court. Didn't matter where he was in the world, he would always be lured by the call of a pickup game even if all he could do was watch.

It was a shame. There were schools and Union Square Park and Madison Square Park, but those weren't places where he and Danny had hung out. They liked the little places, the neighborhood games.

He guessed that was one more thing that had vanished in the age of the internet. Too many kids spending their time online, playing video games, watching hundreds of channels on TV. Such a damn shame.

If he could get Shannon to put her talent to work on the neighborhood, she could transform the whole district. No one whipped up enthusiasm like she did. More importantly, she would love it. He was certain of that. She'd been born to do great things, and while keeping the family together was a fine goal, it only worked if the family wanted to be held together.

He wished, though, that he could be there for her. To encourage her, to make sure she knew every day that she could do anything she set her mind to.

Leaving behind the armory, he headed toward Park Avenue, trying to imagine some clever turn of phrase to tell her she'd been fighting for nothing. That her efforts had been wasted.

Nope, there was no nice way to say any of that. She would be crushed, and he'd be the one to deliver the blow.

SHANNON HAD NO BUSINESS whatsoever meeting Rebecca and Bree for lunch at Brasserie 8½ in Midtown West, but she couldn't stand having so much to say and so few people to say it to.

They'd just finished ordering, and she faced both of her friends from across the booth. "So," she asked, as casual as she could possibly be, "what's new?"

Bree put her hand up in front of her mouth, trying to hide her grin, while Rebecca didn't even bother faking it. She just laughed.

"Please. You're bursting with whatever it is you've got going on." Rebecca Thorpe, who was still in the honeymoon phase of her relationship with her ex-cop, had no compunction about poking Shannon's arm with the back end of her knife. "I have one hour for lunch, and I can't even cheat a little bit. So talk."

"I'm going to be on *WNYC News at Ten* on Thursday night."

Bree and Rebecca both grinned like maniacs. "How come?" Bree asked.

"I'm being interviewed about the Easter egg hunt that my company sponsors in Union Square Park. Well, we're not the only ones who sponsor the festivities, lots of local businesses do, but Fitzgerald and Sons coordinates the event and we put it all together."

"Which means you put it all together," Rebecca said. "But congratulations. This is thrilling. I'm not only going to watch it, I'm going to DVR the whole half hour, then call the station to tell them how impressed I was with the interview. And could I have the name of the beautiful redhead who was in charge?"

"Really?" Shannon asked. Rebecca wasn't just a Thorpe, she was also a Winslow, which in this town meant huge money and incredible influence. Rebecca herself ran the Winslow Foundation, which raised millions for international aid. Huh. She should arrange a dinner with Nate while he was in town. They'd have a lot to talk about.

"Of course, really."

"Why didn't you say something before?" Bree asked. "I didn't know a thing about an Easter egg hunt. How fun. Charlie can put something about the interview in his blog, and then we can do an ad for the event, if that would help."

Shannon took a breath. Then another. She'd never asked her friends to go out of their way for her, even when it was tempting. Charlie, Bree's boyfriend, wasn't an ordinary blogger. He was Charlie Winslow, Rebecca's cousin, and his blog was *Naked New York,* the single most talked-about social-media column in Manhattan.

"That's going way, way above and beyond. I appreciate it so much, but please ask Charlie first. The proceeds all go to feed the homeless and I can send him the information about the charity and how it's run. I don't want either of you to feel obligated."

"We're friends," Rebecca said, leaning over to clasp her hand. "And besides, you deserve everything good for coming up with the trading cards. We both owe you for that."

Shannon held up her water glass, then put it down because the waiter came with the bottle of wine they'd ordered. After he left, she made a proper toast. "To friends and lovers and trading cards."

"And to TV interviews," Rebecca added.

Shannon sipped the very delicious chardonnay and couldn't help but smile. There were wonderful things happening in her life, not the least of which was Nate. The trick there was not thinking too much about how soon he'd be gone.

She felt her mood falter and switched back to focusing on the interview, which with Bree and Rebecca's help she could imagine actually having a big audience. She'd have to be smart, though. Not so self-promoting that she looked as if she didn't care about Easter or the little kids who would be hunting for eggs.

"Oh, God. I'm going to be on TV. With people watching."

"Yes," Bree said. "That's the point."

"Okay. I know it's been done a million times, but I'm going to wear green because it does look best on camera with my hair."

"You look fantastic in green," Bree said. "I have this great tartan skirt that would go so well with that hunter-green blouse that you wore that time when we went for sushi."

"One of your skirts would fit on one of my thighs, but thanks for the offer."

"You always look gorgeous anyway," Rebecca said, just as the waiter brought out their food.

It took a few minutes to deliver the three salads, but soon they were alone. Again Shannon's thoughts returned to Nate and what he would say when she told him the news about Charlie's blog and Rebecca's support. He'd be thrilled for her.

"You know," Rebecca said, turning to Bree, "while the news about the interview is wonderful, why do I have the feeling that our friend Shannon buried the lead?"

"Hmm," Bree said, nodding, ignoring Shannon completely. "I have to agree. The glow? The pink cheeks? The way she's shifting around like she can't sit still?"

"I'd lay odds it's a guy."

"The toast was a dead giveaway," Bree said. "Not just a guy. A trading card guy."

Shannon held up a hand. "Stop. Yes. You're right. I wasn't burying the lead. I was saving the best for last."

Bree shook her head. "I'd say he's one hell of a guy, but that's only because you're blushing so hot you're about to set the tablecloth on fire."

Shannon leaned forward. "His name is Nate Brenner, and he's an architect and urban planner who works in international relief. He's really good-looking, but more importantly he's wonderful. You guys would like him so much. I bet he knows all about the Winslow Foundation, Rebecca."

She smiled. "You mean you haven't spent your nights talking about me and my foundation?" Her friend grinned, put her fork down and held out her hand. "Come on. Out with it."

"What?"

Rebecca sighed. "You know very well exactly what. His card. Let's see it."

Shannon wasn't proud of the fact that she'd stolen his card from the group. Not that she'd change one single thing, but she was still not proud. She opened her purse and took the card out. God, he was gorgeous.

She handed it over to Rebecca, and she could feel her blush intensify.

"Holy cow, he's a hottie," Bree said, as she practically laid over her friend to get a look. "No wonder you kept him to yourself. Look at that smile."

"What organization does he work for?" Rebecca asked.

"The International Rescue Committee."

"That's one of the highest-rated charities in the

world. They do phenomenal work. You say he's an architect?"

"He rebuilds infrastructure in places that have been hit by earthquakes and tsunamis. Mostly in Indonesia and Asia but he thinks that might be changing soon. His home base is in Bali."

Rebecca handed the card to Bree. "Oh, you have got to go see him in Bali," Rebecca said. "Seriously. You'd love it there. It's one of my favorite places on earth."

"He loves it there, too. But there's no way I can go," Shannon said. "Everything at the plant is so tenuous. We're short-staffed as it is. I can't leave the country. I shouldn't even be here."

"It's been like that since I met you," Rebecca said. "There has to be a way you can steal some time for yourself. I'm sure your family would understand."

"I don't know much about what you do," Bree said, not even looking up from his card.

"Run everything but the printing machines, basically. Payroll, taxes. The usual. But most of my time these days is spent on finding new clients."

"It's just your family running the whole thing?"

"We have forty-seven employees. For a couple of years now it's just my father, my brother Brady and me in charge. My mom and my other brothers jumped ship."

"Well, you should figure out a way to take some time off," Bree said, meeting her gaze. "Did you know that when you talk about Nate, your whole face lights up? You really do glow."

"I do?" She put her palms on her heated cheeks. "I've known him all my life. Since we were kids. He's my brother Danny's best friend. But then Nate went away after college and came back all grown up. Gorgeous.

Sweet. Obviously, he's got a tremendous heart. He could be earning buckets running his father's architectural firm, but he doesn't want to live in New York. Or do traditional building."

"How come it says he's a one-night stand?"

"He's leaving as soon as he finishes his business here."

"But his passion is making a difference," Bree said, showing the back of the card to Rebecca, who snatched it up.

"And the bottom line is that he's a sweetheart." Rebecca held up the card as if it was a flag. "A *sweetheart.*"

"He is. He's just not going to be my sweetheart," Shannon said, "at least not forever." She straightened, really hating how her voice had dropped off.

"Ah," the two women across from her said in sync.

"No, it's not like that. I've known all along he's leaving, so it's not a big deal." She sipped her wine, avoiding eye contact.

"You've simply got to go to Bali to visit him," Rebecca said, her voice brooking no arguments. "You owe it to him, and to yourself." She gave the card back, but she'd made her point.

Shannon stared down at his picture, his smile, and she shivered as she remembered the feel of his body so intimately tangled with her own. There was no way in hell she could take the time off to go to Bali.

But she was beginning to think she might not have a choice.

NATE WAS ON THE PHONE WITH George, his direct boss, and the man who was in charge of all projects, excluding fundraising and marketing. George told them all where to go, those who were on the payroll, who were few, and those who consulted or volunteered, who were the real backbone of the IRC. He was also an incredibly nice guy, whom Nate had known since NYU. The man had been responsible for helping Nate find out where he belonged.

"Sumatra is still an issue," Nate said. "They lost so many of their construction people, it's going to be hard for them to pick up the ball and run with it."

"You're going to have to deal with it," George said. "Find someone who can communicate well and we'll make sure you can interface. You've got four more months, Nate, and then we'll need you in Africa."

"No, fine. That's fine. I know we've exceeded our mandate. It's hard to let go."

"I know. The refugee situation has to be dealt with, and all we keep doing is shuffling people from tent city to tent city. These people need something they can call their own. They need to work for themselves and see their labor turn into something real."

"Of course. I'll be wherever you need me." Nate put down his coffee and looked back at the kitchen table, where Shannon was on her laptop doing something that kept her clicking her mouse. She looked so pretty in the morning light, in that pink bathrobe he was going to miss.

"Let me know when you're heading back, yes?"

"I will. Take care, and have Alex send me all the data on where I'll be headed. I need to start planning." Nate disconnected, then went to sit next to Shannon. "What are you so busy working on?"

She turned the laptop so he could see the screen. It was a picture of him surrounded by villagers. He was standing in the middle of a town square, an open air market to his right, a row of sturdy buildings around the perimeter of a small park, with infant trees planted in the general shape of a *Rafflesia arnoldii* flower, the largest flower in the world. That day they had opened the market with great ceremony. It had been scorchingly hot, as wet as the ocean itself, and a day he'd never forget.

"You look so happy," she said. "And so tan."

"Yeah, we didn't have a lot of sunscreen at our disposal. And I was happy. That was a big day."

"But you're not staying there?"

He shrugged. "I go wherever they need me. Which right now is Africa."

"How do you do that? It must be so hard to pick up your life and move it at someone else's whim."

"I don't have a home like you do," he said. "I never did, but I've pared way down. I can carry everything I need in a couple of duffel bags. And everywhere I go, I'm welcome and I'm needed."

"I can see how much you love it."

He almost said, "Just like you love your home," but the thought hurt, the thought of how she didn't know what she was about to be hit with.

Instead he leaned over and kissed her. Long, slow strokes of his tongue, tasting her beneath her coffee, wanting to walk her back upstairs to her bed.

She pulled away first, checking behind him as if they were criminals. It made him want her even more. When her gaze came back to his, she softened, her concern gone knowing they were alone. "I want to hear more about what you do," she said. "I can't now because I have to get ready for work, but I would like to listen. My only frame of reference is 9/11, and how the word *fear* stopped being adequate. How our illusion of safety had been stolen. But there was also the high of coming together. All of New York had been a family, even if it was temporary. You go to those places all the time, and it must be so, so hard, and yet unbelievably satisfying to be part of the solution."

Nate's chest tightened. "It is," he said. "There are horrors and miracles around every corner. Each one breaks my heart. In between is where it gets tricky. I've talked to other relief workers and we all have that sense of disconnect from the ordinary world. We're like soldiers in that respect. It's a limited reality, and it's truly indescribable."

Shannon closed her eyes for a long moment. Took a deep breath. When she opened them again, she smiled. "I've got to go. Busy day ahead. If you're free around three o'clock I've got to go to the park to take some photos. Maybe you'd like to come with?"

"Yeah, sure. Sounds great. I should hear about the offer on the co-op today."

"Oh, exciting. I'm betting it's a yes all the way around." She shut down the laptop and put it under her arm, carrying her coffee in her free hand. He didn't want her to leave, not yet. But she disappeared in a whirl, leaving him to the realization that for all his experience in the face of earthshaking events, he still had absolutely no idea how to help Shannon while still telling her the truth.

13

SHANNON HAD TRIED ON SO many clothes the night before her room now resembled a messy change room at Filene's Basement. It was tempting to call Bree to come help, but in the end she went with her original plan: green blouse that fit her well, slim black skirt, black heels. Tomorrow evening's interview was scarily close, the reality made more terrifying when she'd gotten an email from WNYC about where to go at what time.

The idea that it was live television scared the crap out of her, so she tried not to think about it. But different nightmare scenarios kept popping up: burping in the middle of a sentence, spilling coffee, throwing up, nervously giggling like an idiot. The spectrum of humiliations was huge and varied, but she'd been on stage plenty of times and the butterflies always disappeared the moment she was in the spotlight. Television should be no different.

She got dressed, wishing she had time to put her things in order, but she really did have a packed agenda. She would be sending a massive group email to everyone in her database, asking them to watch the show. She wasn't discriminating about the names, either. Whether they be work related, folks from the church, the St. Marks lunch-exchange crew, family, friends of friends. It was such a large list that she had to break it down into units, or she'd be considered a spammer. Which she supposed she was. But it was for a good cause, so she could live with that.

She also had a meeting with a potential new client this afternoon. Nothing huge, not a lifesaver, but the income would help, and the work was simple. Brochures. Lots and lots of brochures.

Oh, she had to check out *Naked New York* as soon as she got to the office. That would be exciting. She'd send a thank-you card to Charlie and Bree, handwritten, on a card.

The list went on in her head as she did a quick makeup-and-hair check, then she was racing down the stairs. As she turned the corner on the first floor, she bumped into the console table on her way to the coatrack. A file folder fell, spreading a stack of brochures all across the wood floor.

Cursing under her breath, Shannon crouched down and picked up several. They weren't brochures the plant had printed, but rather all about various locales in Florida—Tampa, Orlando, Miami. The file folder wasn't marked, but there was a phone number in the corner written in her mother's hand.

Shannon hadn't realized her folks were thinking about taking a vacation. She should tell them about Bali. It would be good for them to get away. They never went far. They hardly ever took time off at all. An occasional trip to Atlantic City. A weekend at the beach. Good for them for thinking about Florida.

She finished putting everything back, wondering about the brochure for a senior community. She went to open it, noticed the time and shoved everything inside the folder. Then she was off like a shot.

T HE SECOND AFTER N ATE disconnected with Aiko, he pressed Shannon's speed dial.

"Nate."

"Are you at the plant?"

"Yep. Not for long, though. What's up?"

"I'll come get you, and we can go to the park together."

"Okay," she said, and he could hear the smile in the single word. "Give me ten minutes."

"'Bye."

He put his cell in his pocket and raised his arm out to catch a cab. He hit pay dirt a few minutes later and gave the driver the address. It was a short ride from Murray Hill, where he'd been with his accountant since their lunch meeting at noon. The negotiations on the firm were moving at a snail's pace, which wasn't shocking considering the kind of money they were dealing with.

He hated all this crap, but the whole reason he'd come to New York was to get his financial life squared away. He needed enough in his coffers to live without the burden of a traditional job or family. He loved his work, but if he got burned out, which happened with great frequency on the front lines, he wanted to be able to stand on his own. To have insurance, to be able to live where he wanted. He also needed to make sure he was building a future. Maybe someday he'd find someone who fit, who he'd want to settle down with.

Of course he thought of Shannon, but by the time he'd be ready to give up his life, she'd be taken. He was pretty damn stunned she wasn't taken already.

Children weren't in the plans, although, if he thought

he could have a couple of girls with that fantastic red hair… He shook his head. He hadn't wanted children ever, but he did care about a safe retirement. So if it took the lawyers and the moneymen time to work out the deal, so be it.

He was very grateful that his parents had always been smart with money. His mother was set, as was his sister, Leah. The purchase of a co-op apartment had been his accountant's idea, and so far, she'd been an excellent combination of conservative and sufficiently forward-thinking to take reasonable risks.

Shannon would be in good shape, too. In the end. Financially. How she'd be emotionally was a huge unknown. The only thing he knew for sure was that she wouldn't be settled into her new way of life by the middle of May when he had to leave.

The cab turned onto 10th Avenue. He paid the driver, then went inside the building. Shannon was in her office, searching through a stack of papers. She looked up at him and how glad she was to see him was a jolt of adrenaline.

He shut the door. He hadn't seen her since the kitchen. She looked beautiful, as always, but today she'd put her hair up in a smooth ponytail. There should have been another name for the hairstyle because on her it was sleek, elegant and sophisticated. There weren't many women who could carry off that look, but Shannon did.

"Did you hear?"

He blinked at her, trying to figure out— "Oh, yeah. They accepted the offer. Two weeks from Friday on the escrow. The sellers are eager, therefore accommodating."

She dropped the stack in her hands onto her desk

and came to him, her long orange-red ponytail swinging behind her as she walked. Her arms went around him in a tight hug, and it was all he could do not to kiss the daylights out of her. But he didn't know where her dad or Brady were, so...

"I'm thrilled. It won't give you much time to furnish the rest of the— They did agree to include the furniture?"

"Actually, no. It didn't belong to them. So I have to shop from the ground up." The delight on her face made him laugh. "And yes, I'd be very pleased if you could help me with that."

"I've always wanted to do an entire house. This is the best, this is...I can't even start to think about it until next week."

"It'll wait. But we can go back to take measurements, if that helps."

"Yes, yes, of course, it does. What about finding people to sublet? I never asked, did you have someone in mind?"

"Nope, the management company will take care of that."

She kissed him, but only on the chin. Then she stepped back. "We should go. I need to catch the light for the pictures I'm taking. I'm doing a before-and-after of the space for an event bible. So that if I'm not able to coordinate things for any reason, someone can just pick up the book and carry on."

"You are a very smart cookie, have I mentioned that lately?"

"Not nearly often enough, if you ask me."

He nodded. "Noted. You have to do anything, tell anyone before we go?"

"Nope. We're clear."

"You mind if we cab it to 16th and walk the rest of the way?"

"No. Why?"

"I've been in an office or a cab all day. If you're tired, though, it's no big deal."

"I'd love to. My day's been chock-full of stress. A walk will do me good. It's been ages since I've been to the gym."

"You don't need a gym," he murmured. "I'll give you a workout."

Shaking her head in mock disapproval, she led him out to the street, and they walked to 9th Avenue, where they caught a taxi. He held her hand on the ride to West 16th, but they were both quiet—the good kind. They kept sneaking glances at each other, which was silly, but okay, too. He was thirty-two and this thing with Shannon felt like a high-school romance. All the sneaking around. Her parents on the top floor. He didn't mind, although if he had been planning to stay in New York, they would have ended the game by now.

He didn't think her parents would object to him in the long run, but they'd need adjustment time. So would Danny, when it came down to that.

"What's that look?"

He had her hand in his, and they set an easy pace, which made quite a few people tsk at them as if they were tourists. "Trying to imagine what Danny would say if he knew we were together. In the biblical sense."

She gave him a startled look, and he realized that might not have been the right word to use. "He'd have a heart attack, then he'd want you to get your head examined."

"Sounds about right. Although big brothers are supposed to be kind of stupid about their little sisters from what I've heard."

"Mine fit the bill. I'll keel over myself the day they stop calling me Princess."

"It took me a while to realize how very grown-up you are."

"You'd been gone for years. The last memory you had of me was at thirteen. They were here. They were at my graduation. I was a Phi Beta Kappa. That should count for something."

"Why didn't I know that?" he asked.

She shrugged. "I thought Mom let everyone on earth know, but if you'd only been talking to Danny it wasn't the World Series or the Stanley Cup finals, so it wasn't important."

Slipping his arm around the back of her shoulders, he pulled her close. "He can be an idiot, that's for sure. But congratulations. That's an incredible achievement."

"Thank you."

They walked past an empty lot overgrown with weeds, an old dilapidated fence with a fading Keep Out sign doing nothing to prevent a group of tattooed and pierced kids from squatting on junk furniture and makeshift seats. A sight endemic to all big cities, as much a part of New York as the skyline, but it still bothered Nate. Danny accused him regularly of being a bleeding-heart hippie, and Nate had a hard time disagreeing.

"You should bring your IRC crew out here," Shannon said. "Let them take a whack at Manhattan, see what they could do to rebuild and renew."

"The IRC does work out here, but the mandate is different. We help refugees get on their feet, find work and safety."

"That's good," she said. "Important."

He stared as they kept on walking, then turned back to Shannon. "You should seriously consider running for city council."

"In my copious free time?"

"You could do so much good. You're brilliant at organizing, at galvanizing. The Easter thing is a perfect example. I know without a doubt that it's going to bring in tons of money for the homeless, that everyone involved is going to come away from the event happy and that you won't get nearly enough credit for all you've done. See? You're practically a full-fledged council member already."

She squeezed him closer, her hand around his waist. "I've got enough on my plate," she said. "Let me get a few more deep-pocket clients for the plant, then I can relax a little."

He nodded, even as he called himself every kind of coward. But he wasn't going to bring up the family business until after her TV interview. He wouldn't do that to anyone, let alone someone he cared so much about.

They kept walking, slowly, as close as they could be without tripping. "I missed you last night," Shannon said.

"We agreed."

Shannon sighed. "In retrospect, it would have been better if you'd come."

"Tonight, then?"

She nodded, then rested her cheek on his shoulder. "I can't guarantee sexy times. Would that bother you?"

"I'd take sleeping next to you over anything else, hands down. Although I won't be upset if sexy times occur."

They were at the last intersection before the park, and she tugged him around so they faced each other. "This won't take long. The only shots I need are of one area, where the tables and booths will be set up. Then, maybe we could grab a quick dinner. When I get home, I want to go over my bullet list for the interview, get my clothes ready. Nothing very exciting. I plan to be in bed by ten."

He kissed her, a quickie, as there were people in every direction, some very close. "I'll meet you there. Now, if you point me in the right direction, I'll take pictures, too. Anything you need."

She kissed him back, and despite the pedestrians and the traffic, she put her cool palm on the back of his neck to hold him steady as she slipped her tongue between his lips.

She'd just hung up the last of her clothes, the outfit for tomorrow night covered in a dry-cleaner bag. She'd wear the same shoes as she did for work, but her accessories were in a velvet bag in her purse.

It was so much like the old days when she'd lived for being on center stage. The real princess stage of her life had been the pageants, which were only slightly embarrassing. By the time she'd reached her teens she had given up her quest for tiaras and gone after the applause of strangers. She'd been in many school plays, right through her first year of college. She'd have continued for the pure joy of it, but by then she'd accepted that she would join the family business, and she'd focused on her studies.

It was ten o'clock and she needed to get ready for bed. For Nate. As exciting as the interview was, as pressing as the needs of the printing plant were, she'd found herself thinking about Bali or Africa or wherever Nate was going to be. Now that she knew her parents were going to take some time off, she felt less guilty about wanting some for herself.

For ten minutes this afternoon, she'd looked at pictures of Bali. The internet was a wonderful thing, bringing the world to her in her little office. But for once she wanted to go to the world. Despite her best intentions she hadn't been able to stop her traitorous practical mind from taking her to the end of the line. She wished she hadn't seen that picture of him in Sumatra. Before, she'd had vague images in her head about where he lived and worked. Now she couldn't pretend he was anything but temporary, and rightly so.

He was a great man doing great work. A real-life hero. Even in her daydreams she couldn't compete with that. No wonder he thought of her in terms of doing bigger things, like running for city council. Because that's where he lived, in a world where he had a direct impact on the lives of hundreds if not thousands. She had her family and forty-seven employees to take care of. No contest.

She went down the hall to the bathroom, took off her robe and pinned up her hair before she stepped under the shower. The heat and pressure of the water felt incredible, and for a long while she dipped her head, closed her eyes and let her body relax. Tensions had been so high at the office lately that she felt as if it were more of a war zone than a business.

Every effort she made toward easing the stress— bringing doughnuts, making fresh pots of coffee whenever she was there, saying hello, attempting to talk the way they all used to—was met with indifference if she were lucky, barely suppressed antagonism when she wasn't.

Daphne had literally run away from her yesterday. Run, as if to look at Shannon was too painful. Daphne was a few years older than Shannon, and she, along with Melissa, had been really good friends before the cutbacks. They'd often had lunch together, talked about guys and dating and clothes. Before the economy tanked and the layoffs started, she'd invited them to the lunch exchange. Daphne had seemed interested. Now Shannon was the bad guy, the one responsible for everything that had gone wrong at the plant, including the shrinking client base. Shannon had stopped trying to fix what was broken relationship-wise, but she hadn't given up hope that an influx of customers, the type of big clients they used to have, would change everything.

The interview wasn't a guarantee of new business, neither was the Easter egg hunt or the banners or the cold calls or the personal meetings. But there was a chance that it could turn into something major. She was due, dammit, and yes, she understood that was magical thinking. Nevertheless, she would continue to hold on to good thoughts. Positive energy and action combined with a quality product and a track record to be proud of would prove that this was only a temporary downswing. Fitzgerald & Sons had too much history to lose now. She wouldn't let that happen, not under her watch.

She put bodywash on her sponge, her senses filling with lilac and spice, and let all her troubling thoughts run down the drain. In a very short time she would open her door and her bed to the man she wanted more than anything else in the world.

For tonight, she was the luckiest person ever. She couldn't wait until his arms were around her, until she could run her hands down his strong back, feel his breath on her neck, taste him and hear him gasp out her name.

Spurred on by excitement and the ache between her thighs, she rinsed quickly, dried off, brushed her teeth and grinned as she hurried back to her bedroom

She turned on the bedside light, but as a surprise, she'd bought a beautiful pink scarf that she draped over the shade. The room looked exotic and almost as sexy as she felt crawling naked between the sheets.

When he tapped on her door, she tugged down the top sheet so the first thing he saw was her hair spread out on the pillow and her very erect bared nipples. So much for skipping the sexy times.

14

NATE HAD GONE BACK TO HIS room at two that morning, still careful not to upset the applecart, especially today. He'd set his alarm for 5:45 a.m., and after his shower, he'd been glad of it.

Shannon would be down at six-thirty and he wanted her to have more than coffee for breakfast. He'd put on a pair of jeans and a T-shirt and prepared to make the best damn pancakes in all of New York.

The light was already on in the kitchen, which meant Shannon hadn't slept well. He didn't care that his surprise was screwed up as much as the fact that she was starting the day out nervous. Only it wasn't Shannon in the kitchen, but Mrs. Fitz.

"What are you doing up so early, boyo?"

He walked in to the scent of freshly brewed coffee and butter melting on a grill pan. "I came to make pancakes for the TV star."

Mrs. Fitz grinned. "That was very nice of you."

"And you," he said, as he got his mug down from the cupboard.

"She's so excited. She'd tried to get every station in New York to advertise the fundraiser, and no one's ever taken notice. It's a fine thing, her efforts paying off so well."

"Yeah," he said. "She works hard for the church. For everything she loves."

Mrs. Fitz put a ladle's worth of batter on the griddle, bringing vanilla and cinnamon into the delicious mix of aromas. "I know what Danny's asked you to do."

He stirred his coffee, then went to the table. "I wasn't sure."

"We're in a terrible position," she said. "We've done it to ourselves, and now we're asking you to fix it. Shameful. I'd speak to her myself if I had the courage God gave a ten-year-old. She's my little girl, and this situation is breaking my heart."

"I understand," Nate said. "But she's got to know the truth. It'll work out, I'm sure of it, but it's not going to be easy for any of you. I can't say I'm glad to help, but I'm the right person for the job."

Mrs. Fitz, still in bathrobe and slippers, had poured out four cakes, and she was watching them for the first of the bubbles. Syrup, the real kind, was at the ready, and there were four place settings on the table. "It's kind of you, Nate. We've all noticed how you two are thick as thieves. That's good. That's wonderful. You're family, and she can use the company. She works too hard, that one. I hope..."

"What?"

She flipped all four pancakes, then glanced at him before facing the stove once more. "I hope she lands on her feet. That's what frightens me the most. She's so talented and bright, but it never seemed to matter how often we told her she could do anything at all, chase any dream, she was convinced that the business came first. That we all lived and died for the bloody printing plant.

I'm grateful for it, God knows, it's kept us in food and clothing and our home for all these years, but if I never set foot in that place again, it'll be too soon.

"Mr. Fitz is deaf in one ear, did you know that? And the hearing in the other ear isn't good. He's tired, and he's ready for a full retirement without the worry. We all are. Shannon deserves her own life, cut off from any obligations, real or imagined. I want her to be happy, Nathan. I want her to be free."

He stared at his coffee, wishing he could skip the painful part, the part where Shannon would be crushed by the betrayal. But he couldn't. "You'll need to tell her that in a while," he said. "You'll need to say it many times, I think. She won't believe it at first. She'll just be angry. Worse, she'll feel like a fool."

Mrs. Fitz filled his plate and brought it over to the table. After setting it down, she placed her hand on his shoulder. "I'm sorry to bring you into this," she said. "But we're all grateful for you being there to help us through it."

He covered her hand with his. "We're family," he said. "I love you guys."

"Shannon'll be down in a minute. Eat up. You're far too thin."

Today was going to be wonderful for Shannon. She deserved the spotlight, the attention. She deserved the best he had to offer.

THE DAY WENT BY IN FITS and starts. Shannon's butterflies would swoop around and she'd fixate on the potential for failure, then some bit of work would catch her notice. Rinse. Repeat. It was only two o'clock. She was due at the studio at eight. She'd decided to eat her lunch at midafternoon, because she didn't want to have a blood-sugar crash, but she also had to account for the nerves. She'd brought soup, crusty bread, a banana.

Now she wanted chai tea, which they had only in the big break room. She left the quiet of her office, putting in her earplugs as she walked. Across the floor, she saw Melissa, Greg and Patrice huddled around someone in a chair. Shannon raced over to find out what was going on.

There were accidents from time to time; it was a big plant with lots of machinery, but it had been a while since anyone had been injured. Brady ran a tight ship, and there were frequent enough breaks so that no one would get too drowsy at the controls. Oh, God, she could see now that it was Daphne, and she had her face buried in her hands, shaking, crying. What the hell?

Patrice saw Shannon first and the expression on her face, such incredible contempt, made her flush. It was awful being the object of scorn, of mistrust. She was hated and no amount of explanations seemed to change anyone's mind.

Greg and Melissa were staring at her now, and they backed away from Daphne, who continued to weep. Shannon crouched in front of Daphne's chair, touched her knee. Daphne glanced up, her mouth opened as if gasping, and she rose so swiftly she almost knocked Shannon on her ass.

Daphne darted past her coworkers, heading toward the back of the shop, Shannon right on her tail. There was no way she could ignore this or even send Brady to investigate. She didn't know if Daphne had been injured or if something else was tearing her apart.

Daphne rushed into the ladies' room. By the time Shannon went inside, her ex-friend was shutting a cubicle door behind her. Shannon's right hand pressed back, and she yanked out her earplugs with her left. "Daphne, wait."

"Go away."

"I can't. Please. Tell me if you're hurt."

"No. I'm fine. Just go away."

"You're not fine," Shannon said. "I hate this. Please, let's just talk. I know it's been rocky between us, but—"

The pressure on Daphne's side of the door vanished, and Shannon stumbled forward, barely able to stop herself before she plowed into Daphne. Straightening quickly, Shannon took several steps back.

Daphne didn't seem to have noticed either the stumbling or Shannon's attempt to give her some breathing room. "Rocky?" she repeated, as if Shannon had spit the word at her. "Things have been rocky? Do you know what the insurance company wants to charge for catastrophic illness coverage? More than my monthly paycheck, that's what. Because I was born with diabetes. I've stopped sleeping, I'm going to lose my apartment, and then what? All I know how to do is work the printing machines, and there are no jobs out there. None."

She took a step toward Shannon, her face blotchy and her eyes red. She pointed her finger like a weapon as she shouted, "Why don't you just do it already. You think we're stupid? That we don't know?"

"Do what? Know what?"

Daphne's face twisted into such an ugly mask it made Shannon feel sick. "Yeah, you do think we're idiots. Working twice as hard for less money. Doing the job of three and four people. No insurance, and your father is all about planning his retirement so he can go sit on a beach somewhere and have fancy drinks. Brady's got a drawer full of brochures about new and better places to work. We know that guy that came by last week with your dad was a buyer. You all are going to walk away millionaires, and we'll be shit out of luck without a nickel."

"What are you talking about?" Shannon had to grip the sink behind her. The tirade was insane, it made no sense. "My father's not retiring. We're not trying to sell anything. I'm doing everything in the world I can to bring us more clients. Why do you think I've been working so hard on this Easter project? I'm trolling for customers. I spend half my day making cold calls. Would I do that if we were trying to sell the plant?"

Daphne wiped her nose with a tissue, then crossed her arms defensively. "Fine. Great. And I was feeling all guilty, but now I— You'll just keep feeding us this bullshit until we're all so desperate, we quit, and you won't have to pay severance."

"What? No. That's not true."

Daphne looked over Shannon's shoulder, and Shannon followed her gaze. The entrance to the ladies' room was filled with the other employees, and it was clear they hadn't believed a word she said.

"I've never lied to you." Shannon stood up straight, rallied her dignity. "It's been a struggle for everyone. All I've been working toward is keeping the plant going. Getting back on our feet so we can rehire a full crew. The decision to cut the insurance came down to the wire. It was that, or close the doors for good. You know that. I told you that. I give you my word, we're not trying to sell the building. Why would we? It's been in our family for generations."

Daphne laughed. "You know what? I don't feel so good. I think I'll take a paid sick day." She put her hand in front of her mouth. "Oh, wait. Those were cut down to two days every six months. I don't have any left."

Shannon opened her mouth to keep trying, but Daphne shut the cubicle door. The staff didn't leave, but they did part to let her through. It was torturous, walking that gauntlet of mistrust and anger. She wasn't everyone's favorite person, but she'd never been hated before. Not even for things that she had done wrong.

Why did they all think she was lying? The confrontation had been a nightmare, her worst fears shouted in her face.

It had to be terrifying to have a chronic illness and not have insurance. Scary to have no real job security. But that was how it was now, not just at Fitzgerald & Sons. At least they had jobs. The plant had never missed a single payroll, not once. Shannon knew other companies were eliminating sick pay altogether.

She went back to her office, staring straight ahead. She wanted to leave, to find Nate, to fall into his arms and have him tell her that things couldn't have gotten this messed up.

She locked her door, closed the blinds. Tears threatened, but she wouldn't give in, not today. Not when she was busting her ass to keep all the employees. Daphne wasn't the only one who wasn't sleeping.

Her screensaver mocked her with pictures of happier times in the plant. Birthday parties, potlucks, costumes on Halloween. This had always been a great place to work, and it could be again. If only the staff were willing to have a little faith. But they weren't. After all these years, all the effort and the stress. They obviously hadn't bothered to think about the family's side of the equation.

She sniffed, opened her purse to get out her face powder, but took out Nate's trading card instead. She smiled at him and at the fact that she still carried his card around with her. She thought of calling, but he was in meetings until this evening when he was going to watch her interview along with half the neighborhood at Molly's.

That was the good side of living someplace forever. With the obvious exception of their employees, the Fitzgeralds meant something in Gramercy. They were honorable people. Her family had taught her to tell the truth, to value a job well done, to treat people with respect.

Time to focus again on Nate and let his picture bring her blood pressure down. It was coming on three o'clock. She had work to do, as always. Cold calls, mostly, but some filing, emails to answer. There was very little chance those things would be accomplished if she didn't lift herself out of this funk. So she'd take her lunch, a whole damn hour, and she'd go for a walk. Walking always helped. Then she'd come back to the office, and she'd do her job.

Tonight she'd put on her favorite outfit, brush her hair, freshen her lipstick and she'd smile when she got on camera. She'd talk about the fun they would have on Easter Sunday after mass. How each donation would help people who were truly in need. She refused to be in a bad mood when she had no power to change the outcome. She was doing her best. Working as hard as she knew how.

She was not a failure, and she wasn't going to act like one.

THE BUILDING WAS STEEL AND glass, and it didn't look like a television studio lived inside, but she'd never been to one before, so that made little sense. It had taken Shannon over an hour on the subway to arrive at the studio in Yonkers. She'd used the time to gear herself up, to let the earlier part of the day go as she focused not on the opportunity to promote Fitzgerald & Sons, but on the altruistic purpose of the Easter egg hunt itself.

Inside she was given a badge, and an escort, a harried young woman named Felicity, took her into a tiny little makeup area where someone who barely acknowledged Shannon powdered her face within an inch of its life. Felicity then took her to the green room, which wasn't green and didn't smell nice, either. The monitor that would have let her watch the broadcast was down, needing to be replaced, so Felicity pointed out a stack of old magazines. Shannon would be the only in-studio guest for the evening.

As soon as she was alone, she brought out her phone and called Nate.

"Hey," he said, his voice as comforting as a hug. "How you doing?"

"Fine," she said. "Nervous."

"You're a natural. They'll probably ask you to be their next anchor."

She laughed a bit, a first for the day, and debated telling him about what had happened at work. The decision was made a second later as she really couldn't afford to get caught up in any drama. It was disappointing, though, to realize that her pep talk had given her only a veneer of equilibrium.

"Tell me about your meetings," she said.

"They were about as dull as meetings get."

"I don't care. I don't want to think about being on camera. So you need to entertain me. You're at Molly's, right?"

"I am. It's packed. Everyone's here. Even people I

used to know. Mrs. Gailbraith from four doors down is here."

"What? She never goes out. Did you thank her for all those candy bars?"

"I did. Told her she was the best Halloween house on the whole block. She seemed pleased."

"What about the family?"

"Myles and Alice are here, so are Brady and Paula. Danny's come with a very beautiful girl who's far too good for him— Ow."

Shannon was smiling now for real. She knew instantly that Nate had made that last crack within hearing range of Danny, who had proceeded to exact immediate revenge.

"Princess!" It was Danny himself on the phone now. "Ow. Jesus, Nate, take my shoulder off, why don't you." Danny added a muttered expletive. "Hey," he said into the phone. "Is it true you don't want to be called Princess anymore?"

"Yes." She let out a happy sigh. Nate would get a bonus tonight for that. "Who's your friend?"

"She's a gorgeous woman of discriminating taste, and you'll meet her when you come back to visit the little people."

She shook her head. "As always, Danny, you're a riot. Is Tim there?"

"Yeah. He and Brady are arm wrestling. For money."

"Don't let Ma catch them."

"She's already made ten bucks, are you kidding?"

"Give me back to Nate, you hooligan."

It took a moment for the phone to get into Nate's hand, and then he told her to hang on. When he spoke again, the background was much quieter. "I'm back. It's a madhouse out here."

"Watch, I'll probably do something horribly embarrassing. Get the hiccups or something."

"No, you won't. And even if you did, we'd love you just the same."

She knew he was talking about the family, about love in the broadest sense, but that didn't stop the flurry that kicked up inside her. "I'm going to splurge after this and take a cab home."

"Good. I was about to suggest that. I was worried about you on the subway."

She wished he was there with her, not at Molly's. "I can take care of myself, but I'm tired, and I want to be at home."

"Tonight's going to be rough," he said, his voice lower, a little harder to hear. "The gang's all staying over."

"I figured. Maybe you can sneak in when everyone's asleep."

"Or maybe I could steal you away, and we could spend the weekend at a hotel."

She sighed. "That sounds—"

Felicity opened the door. "You're up."

"I've got to go," Shannon said, as the butterflies in her stomach suddenly grew teeth.

"Break a leg," he said.

"Thanks. 'Bye."

Felicity barely glanced at her as she led her through corridors, over great big cables that were strewn about on the floor. There were flashing red Silence signs all along the way, and as they got closer to where the action seemed to be, the signs changed to On Air.

There were cameras, two of them, and the cohosts' desks. The set itself seemed incredibly smaller than it looked on television. She recognized Lisa Jenner at one desk, a very large picture of the New York skyline behind her, talking to the camera, reading from a Tele-PrompTer. She seemed relaxed and pretty, never once looking down at the papers that were in front of her.

Grant Yost was at the second desk, the one Shannon was escorted to. It had a swirled blue backdrop with the station's call letters in white. To his right, out of camera range, Shannon saw herself and Grant in a very large monitor. Her hair looked okay, but she should have gone with the matte lipstick. She was seated in a chair that had a low back. Since Lisa was still speaking, no one gave her any instructions, but she assumed that would come in a moment.

Sure enough, the red light on the camera went off, and before Shannon could introduce herself to Grant, Felicity got her attention. As she fit Shannon with a tiny clip-on microphone, she said, "Look at Grant, not the camera. Seriously, looking at the camera ends up being creepy."

Shannon took out the flyer for the Easter egg hunt. "Who should I give this to?"

Felicity looked at the paper blankly, then said, "I'll take care of it. You'll be on in five."

Five didn't mean minutes, but seconds. Grant still hadn't looked at her when he faced the camera. "Tonight's guest is Shannon Fitzgerald of Fitzgerald and Sons Printing. They're famous for making trading cards for the New York Yankees and the New York Mets, to name two famous franchises. They also print textbooks and catalogues and even children's books. What WNYC has recently discovered, however, is that Fitzgerald and Sons also prints a different type of trading card."

A picture replaced the live shot of her and Grant. Shannon stared in mute horror at Nate's trading card,

surrounded by five other cards, all the men from the
last batch she'd taken to the St. Marks lunch exchange.

"These cards aren't keepsakes. They're solicitations.
Traded among a prominent group of women including,
it appears, Rebecca Winslow Thorpe, CEO of the ven-
erable philanthropic Winslow Foundation."

A video of Rebecca, Bree and Katy came up in the
nightmarish slide show, walking into the church, with
Rebecca looking behind her as if she were doing something illegal. Shannon's mouth opened. Inside her head
she screamed for Yost to stop but she couldn't seem to
make a sound.

"The men on these cards," Grant continued, "have
no idea they're being traded like so much chattel."

Grant shifted his attention to Shannon. "Ms. Fitzgerald, I understand you were the person who came up with
this trading scheme several months ago, and since then,
over a hundred unsuspecting New Yorkers have been
up for auction in the basement of St. Marks Church. Is
it true that a percentage of each sale goes directly into
your pocket?"

15

SHANNON COULDN'T BREATHE. The room spun and she had to grab on to the desk to keep herself upright. "I don't understand," she said. "What about the Easter egg hunt?"

"Please, Ms. Fitzgerald. Explain to us how this trading card system works. How you've managed to keep the scheme quiet for so long. I was told there's a strict confidentiality agreement among the women who sign up to be involved with the auction?"

"There's no auction. It's not like that. We're friends. It's for fun, and for connections between friends."

"If it were for fun, then why weren't the men who are being traded asked if they wanted to participate? If it were as innocent as you claim, why would so many of the men on the back be marketed as One Night Stands?"

Nate's picture was still on the backdrop, but next to it now was the picture of the back of his card. One Night Stand written in bold.

Shannon felt as if she were going to be sick. "There's no auction, no money. It was meant as something nice. Something good."

"Tell that to the men you've been swapping."

She knew she had to explain, get him to listen and stop making horrible accusations. But Nate was watching this show. Her family and everyone she knew were watching this show, and she hadn't asked. She'd used Nate, and all the other men, and she hadn't asked. How could she have not seen how intrusive…?

"None of this was done maliciously or for profit," she said, trying with all her heart to be as professional as she could. The humiliation was strangling her, but she had to keep on. "We're all friends. We share lunches. And we talk about dating and how hard it is in New York—"

"So you saw an opportunity and you ran with it. Using the printing plant. Did your family know you were printing trading cards with such personal information? One card we saw said, and I quote, 'He's so hot, you'll need a fire extinguisher.'"

"You're taking everything out of context. That's how girls talk about potential dates. It's not wrong." Her voice caught, and she knew her face was red, which made her want to double over and die.

"I think you'll find the men on these cards, and we have yet to quantify exactly how many that is, will have something to say about whether it was wrong to use their pictures, their personal information, to barter them without their express permission." Grant turned to the camera, and Shannon caught sight of the monitor. Nate was center stage, as if he represented all kinds of horrible and salacious things done in secret basement meetings.

"We'll have more on this story in the coming weeks as we uncover how many men have been secretly shared among this group of women under the guise of trading lunches. We'll return in a moment."

The red light on the camera turned off, and Grant calmly removed the microphone hidden under his tie. He didn't look at her. Not once. He got out of his seat and walked over to some woman standing by the exit.

Shannon forced herself out of her seat. She took the microphone she'd been given, dropped it on the floor and stepped on it as hard as she could as she followed signs out of the building. Someone called her name, a man, whom she ignored.

Where had they gotten their information? She trusted every last woman at the lunch group. No one would have blabbed. Not only were they all trustworthy, but publicizing the cards ruined everything for everyone. So who…?

"Oh, God." She braced a hand on the wall. She knew…she knew…

The day she'd been working on Nate's card, she'd gone for coffee and when she'd come back, the picture of the abandoned printing plant had been on her screen. That's when someone had downloaded the batch of cards.

She knew who that someone was, and that hurt almost as much as the blinding humiliation. Daphne. Shannon pressed a hand to her stomach.

Daphne had been to Shannon's home. She knew her family. The two of them had shared more stories about dates than Shannon ever had with any member of the exchange. Daphne had been her friend.

Then again, Shannon was Nate's friend, and what had that gotten him?

NATE WAS STILL STARING AT THE big television behind the bar at Molly's. The packed room had gone silent, the TV

muted. He was squeezing his beer glass so hard, either
it would shatter or his fingers would break. *Shannon.*

It had been a shock to see his picture on the screen.
Trading cards? He'd always dreamed about being on a
card, practically every boy he'd known had wanted that,
but for sports. For being famous. Nate had no idea what
to make of the card he was on. One thing he knew for
certain was that Shannon hadn't done anything wrong.
That two-bit hack of a news anchor had been full of it.

The other thing he was sure about was that Shannon had been eviscerated. Tricked, shanghaied, humiliated, three days before her charity Easter egg hunt. Nate
wasn't a violent man, but he would personally strangle
whomever had planted that story.

He would also call his old buddy Brent first thing in
the morning. Brent was one of the best litigators in the
country.

"What the hell was that?"

At Danny's bewildered question, Nate jerked out
of revenge mode. He didn't answer, but it did get him
pressing her speed dial number. Her cell rang and rang,
until it went to voice mail. "Shannon. I'll call you back.
Pick up, honey. Please. It'll be okay, but I need to know
where you are."

He hung up, hit redial. Got the same result. She
hadn't turned off the phone, then, but she wasn't an-
swering. The next three times he called, the number was
busy. So he wasn't the only one calling. He hoped it was
friends, but for all he knew, there could be other news
media trying to get in on the story. Rebecca Thorpe was
involved, and that was big news. Very big.

"I can't get through," Mrs. Fitz said.

"Me, neither," Nate said, swallowing hard.

Mrs. Fitz looked wild-eyed. "She's all the way in

Yonkers. She'll be beside herself. We have to go get her."

"She told me she was going to take a cab home," Nate said. He would have hugged Mrs. Fitz himself if Mr. Fitz wasn't already holding her.

Every person Nate saw looked shell-shocked. He felt the same. The accusations that bastard had flung about had been disgusting. To blindside Shannon without giving her the chance to defend herself was the worst kind of sensationalism with no regard for the truth. He didn't give a damn if his picture ended up on every news show in America, he would not have Shannon treated like that.

He was shaking in his rage, with his worry. She was out there, an hour away at least, and if she didn't pick up the phone, he didn't know what he was going to do.

She had been so frightened of things going wrong. The hiccups. Jesus. The bar was too hot, too crowded, and he thrust his way out.

The night was supposedly the coldest in weeks, but he didn't feel it. Adrenaline made his heart pound, made him want to jump in the next cab and race to her side. He had no idea how to find her. Someone could probably trace the GPS in her phone, but not anyone he knew.

"Shit," he said, and he said it again because he could. He was going to find out where that prick Grant lived and make him sorry he was ever born. Nate dialed again, and when he got the busy signal he almost threw the cell as far as he could launch it. With an effort, he held back. Barely. He didn't know what to do with himself. Except worry. And think the worst.

SHANNON WAS ON THE SUBWAY. She wasn't sure which train or where it was headed. She'd just used her Me-troCard and climbed aboard the first open door she saw.

She'd shredded a number of tissues and stuffed the remains in her purse. There were two clean ones left. She might have to buy more because she wasn't getting off this train. Ever.

She was sitting on a side bench, holding on to a pole, staring out the window as the tunnel flashed by. Oddly, she felt as if she'd left herself on a chair in a TV studio where the world she used to know had been crushed out of existence. She had no idea who was riding this near-empty subway car.

Thankfully, it was after eleven. Not too many people out and about at this time, not like rush hour. Still, New York never really shut down, so she wouldn't be alone no matter what. Too bad.

She closed her eyes and just as quickly opened them again. It was the fourth time she'd tried and she wouldn't try again. Closing her eyes didn't provide enough distractions. Behind closed eyes she would remember not any particular word, but a tone, the way it felt when she realized exactly what he was accusing her of.

All her work, all the struggle, the effort, the calls, the nights she couldn't sleep worrying about Fitzgerald & Sons—all of it was for nothing. They were a joke now. It didn't matter how the story ended. Even if by some miracle the reporter apologized for his misinformation on the air, it wouldn't be enough. People's memories were short, and with a shocking story like this one, that's all they'd need.

No one would think of Fitzgerald & Sons without the association of Shannon Fitzgerald running some underground man swap. She didn't even know what that meant, except that it was salacious and filthy. That's all her customers would think. As they canceled their orders.

How could she ever make another cold call? How could she assure the potential customers who were on the brink of signing? Credibility, gone. Self-respect, none. And they'd used Nate as the symbol of her disgrace.

Damn, now she was down to one tissue. She had money. Credit cards. She supposed she could get out at the next stop, find herself a place to hide for the night.

No, no, not a hotel. She would never sleep. At least here there were people coming and people going. All of them looked as if their world hadn't been shredded.

God, they'd shown Rebecca. How many times had they sat outside St. Marks shooting footage, trolling, hoping to find the right person or shot? How long would it take for someone to recognize Bree as Charlie Winslow's girlfriend then make their connection to the cards? Shannon couldn't even imagine the backpedaling they'd have to do.

She bent over, holding her stomach, biting her lip to keep from moaning out loud. Charlie had no idea about the cards. Rebecca's boyfriend, Jake, had been wounded in the line of duty in the NYPD, and now he'd be a laughingstock, and it was all Shannon's fault.

At least Nate was leaving New York. Not soon enough to outrun the ridicule that would come at him from all corners. Shannon had used every weapon in her arsenal to make sure the interview was watched by everyone who had even a tangential relationship to the Fitzgerald family or the business. She'd even figured out when affiliates of the tiny independent station would rerun the piece, and had sent alternative times and channels to all her address books.

God, with every stop and start of the subway a new horror came to haunt her. The repercussions to the lunch exchange women! Their families, their coworkers, all the men they'd ever dated. The circle kept growing and growing. How was her mother ever going to walk into church again? The Easter egg hunt!

Shannon sat up, but she was breathing too fast, and if she didn't get herself under control she was going to hyperventilate and pass out, and wouldn't that make a lovely picture for the *Post.*

It took two transfers and a dozen or more stops to finally reach Grand Central. Shannon could get tissues. Could find a train to anywhere. She'd heard rumors that people lived underground, in the station in abandoned train tunnels. That might not be so bad. Although she'd need a toothbrush. And more practical shoes.

The doors whooshed open and she stepped out. She walked. The four-faced clock was straight ahead. Shannon looked up and smiled. At last, something that made sense. The sky was backward on this ceiling. She'd come here with her fifth-grade class, and her teacher, Mr. Thomas, had made a very big deal of the backward ceiling. He'd said it was supposed to be the sky as God would see it.

According to all four faces of the clock, it was very late. She'd been riding the trains for hours, and somehow it had become 2:00 a.m.

She found her last tissue and kept on walking.

NATE SAT ON THE FITZGERALDS' porch steps, leaning against a post, freezing cold. They'd left the outside light on for when Shannon came home. If Shannon came home.

In all the places he'd been across the globe where

people had been desperate to find loved ones, Nate's role had been to be calm, supportive, gentle. He'd been the person they'd turned to for comfort.

Tonight he was the desperate soul, the one panicked beyond reason. The truth was the comfort he'd offered overseas had been useless. The hot coffee or the blankets had been all that mattered. His calm support had only helped him, not them.

He didn't know how to find her. Shannon was out there, and anything could have happened. He'd run through a hundred scenarios, all of them ending in tragedy. It was torture. For hours, every moment that went by was the moment before she would appear. When Molly's had emptied, only staff and Shannon's family remaining, he'd been certain she'd left a message on the machine at the house, only to have Mrs. Fitz remind him that Brady and his girlfriend had gone home hours before, just in case.

Nate had paced and dialed her cell until her voice mail had no more room. Now, as he sat in the cold, gripping his cell phone so tightly he bruised his hand, he was bargaining. If she came home, he'd never say a word to her about how she'd turned him into a trading card.

He would have preferred that the story hadn't already gone viral on the internet. Evidently, the Winslow family was big news everywhere. One of them was running for senator. Danny had shown Nate the story on Yahoo. A quick Google search had links to everything from the Winslow wiki to the history of trading cards, male prostitution, which had been a body blow, and the entire interview on YouTube.

But he didn't care. He wouldn't say a word because he knew she hadn't meant to hurt any of them. He'd only really gotten to know her in the past couple of weeks, but he was absolutely certain that this trading card thing was her attempt to help her friends find love. That's all. Because that's what Shannon did. She helped people—strangers, friends, family, community. The gorgeous redhead didn't have a malicious bone in her body, and God only knew how she was dealing with this avalanche of lies and blame.

He'd give up pretty much everything so that she wouldn't have to go through this pain, and that was a body shock of a different kind.

He hadn't realized until this morning, until he was alone waiting on the steps, that things had gone way beyond friends who have sex. He'd been convinced for years now that he wouldn't have to worry about the consequences of love. Wrong. So wrong. And with, of all people, the Princess.

He thought about going inside. He wouldn't go to bed, that was out of the question, but he could use something hot to drink. It was after 3:00 a.m., and his panic had been cycling for so long it felt as if he'd never relax again.

Then he heard footsteps. The click of heels on the sidewalk. He didn't move, didn't dare breathe in case he jinxed it or scared her off. If it was her.

It had to be her.

More steps, steps slowing down. It was Shannon. The relief hit him so hard he nearly passed out. Then he saw her face as she looked up at her home. His chest seized at the sorrow. At her hopelessness. Her pain and her guilt were written in her skin. Her eyes… Jesus. This was a woman gutted.

She shook her head, pressed the heels of her palms

against her eyes, then turned away, took a step to leave again.

Nate was on his feet in a second. "Don't."

Shannon gasped as her hand went to her chest.

"Don't you walk away," he said, running down the few stairs until he could grip her by the shoulders, hold her in place. He didn't even care that his cell phone was still in his hand, he was not letting go. "Do you have any idea how worried I've been? How worried we've all been? Your mother's beside herself. You didn't answer your phone. It's goddamn three in the morning, and anything could have happened to you. Anything."

She opened her mouth, but all that came out was a squeak.

"You can't do that to me again, you hear me?"

"Why?" she said finally, her voice high and lost. "How can you even look at me? I've done everything wrong. I made a laughingstock of you. Of the plant. I've ruined *everything*."

"You're remarkable, but not even you could ruin everything."

Shannon pushed at him weakly. "There's nothing funny about this. I'm a disgrace and Fitzgerald and Sons is going to pay for it. That terrible anchorman used your picture, and I lied to you about that. I didn't put your picture in the Gramercy newsletter, I used it to get you dates, and then I stole the card so no one could date you but me, but I never asked you, and that was horrible. You have every reason to hate me for it. And now I've dragged Rebecca into the mud, and she didn't do anything wrong. All my friends, they were just playing along with me, but the trading cards were my idea. My fault. And I made sure everyone kept it a secret. I had to have known it was wrong or I wouldn't have cared that it was a secret." She took in a deep breath, and when she let it out her whole body sagged.

He pulled her close, right up against his chest.

"I'm so sorry," she said, and he felt her body tremble, her shoulders shake with her weeping. "I'm so sorry."

Nate closed his eyes and rocked her, using his free hand to gently stroke her hair, giving her as much comfort as he could. But all he kept thinking was how grateful he was that she was alive. That she was here. That he could hold her.

That he loved her.

16

"YOU READY?" HE ASKED, as he lifted her chin.

Shannon shook her head. "As soon as they realize I'm not dead, they'll remember what I've done."

"You haven't done anything. Your family needs to know you're all right. I can't imagine even one of them is sleeping."

"No."

"Yeah, and trust me. Every moment is torture, so buck up."

She couldn't believe she'd have to face them when she was this tired and fragile. But since her feet had brought her home without her permission, she supposed it was inevitable. People didn't actually die from shame. They just wished they had. "All right. Let's go."

He had his arm around her shoulders, and she slipped hers around his waist. Nate's effort got them up the stairs. He put his hand on the doorknob, but kissed her temple before he used it. "It'll be okay," he said, as he took her inside.

There were lights on in the living room and the kitchen, and the moment the front door closed, Shannon heard her mother cry out. Then it was bedlam.

Her mother and father, hurrying from the kitchen, her mom holding an empty cup. Brady, Danny, Myles, Alice and Tim all came thundering from the living room and upstairs. Finally Paula, whom Shannon had met only twice, came stumbling down, tying her robe around her middle.

"Where have you been?" her mother asked. "We've been frantic. God in heaven." She pulled Shannon away from Nate and into her arms. "Never do that again, young lady. You aged us ten years with that disappearing act. Never again."

When Shannon was released, it was for only a second, and then her father took her up in a bear hug. He'd never been the type for hugs, and it was weird to feel him shaking, to feel the strength of his emotion. "Jesus Christ," he said. "You scared the life out of us."

The brothers just stared at her, for which she was more than grateful. When her father let go, she stepped back until she felt Nate at her side. "I'm sorry I made you all worry," she said. "And I'm sorry for the incredible mess I've gotten us all into. I never meant any harm. I don't know why they thought I was taking money or doing anything unsavory with the cards, but that's not the point. The fact is, I did use the printing plant for my own reasons. To make trading cards for my friends at the lunch exchange. I never did ask any of the men for their permission. That was wrong, and I'll apologize to each and every one.

"Mostly, I'm sorry for the damage I've done to Fitzgerald and Sons. I've humiliated us all. I don't know what's going to happen. People are bound to believe what they've heard on the news, even if it is just WNYC. I've tried so hard to keep our good name in front of the public, and now we're a joke, an embarrassment, and that's all my fault."

"It's…a little more than WNYC," Danny said.

"What? What's happened now?"

"I'm sorry, Prin—Shannon," Danny corrected himself and smiled, and that alone almost made her start crying again. "But the internet got wind. Because of Rebecca Thorpe. The story's out there."

Nate's arm went around Shannon's shoulders again, and he gave her a squeeze. "There are things we can do after we've all had some sleep. A retraction, for one thing. That son of a bitch Grant Yost is looking at a hell of a slander suit, and that's just from my attorney. I can't imagine what Rebecca Thorpe's going to do to him."

"But I didn't get permission."

"If you think that there's a single straight man out there who wouldn't agree to being on one of your trading cards, then you need to get out more."

Shannon blinked up at him. "But—"

"Am I on a card?" Danny asked.

"No," she said, not understanding his tone. He should have been outraged at the thought.

"Why not? What, I'm not good enough for your lunch exchange?"

She stared at her brother, wondering if she were hallucinating. "You'd want me to put you on a card?"

"Hell, yeah. Especially one of those one-night-stand numbers. Wouldn't that make life easier. Everything right out in the open."

"I'd get in on that action," Tim said. "You know all these women, right? There are no scary ones? I met this woman through an online dating service, and she turned out to be a stalker. She wanted to get married on our second date."

"That doesn't make her a stalker," Myles said.

Danny poked Tim with his elbow. "That makes her crazy. Wanting an ugly idiot like you."

"Hey, you're one to talk."

"Hold it," Nate said, his voice carrying over the room. "It's late. Tomorrow we can talk about everything. Sleep is the next order of business."

Shannon's mom turned to face her boys. "You all go on. Get to your rooms. Myles and Alice, don't worry about Nate. He's going to be bunking elsewhere."

"Where's that?" Nate asked, taking a step away from Shannon.

Her mother looked Nate in the eyes. "Your choice. The couch in the living room is comfortable. But you might as well go on and be with Shannon. Mr. Fitz and I appreciate your consideration, but given the circumstances, we're prepared to keep on pretending we don't know a thing."

NATE GRABBED HIS STUFF from Myles's room, then hurried to Shannon's. He thought about getting his bathroom business out of the way, but he didn't want to leave her on her own until she was safely in bed.

Good thing he came back because while she'd managed to get her shoes off, she was having trouble with her blouse. Her exhaustion ran so deep she could barely control her fingers enough to undo the top button.

Nate stepped in to help. Her hands dropped to her sides the second he touched her. Her eyes kept closing and opening until the blouse was undone and pulled out of her skirt. It was like undressing a wobbly mannequin. He'd raise her arm, and it would sink back down before the sleeve was off. He ached with how woozy and pale she was. Eventually he removed her blouse and quickly slipped off her bra. Taking off her panties was faster, and he felt as if he'd won something when she was finally naked.

God. She fell against him, and he held her, knowing he should help her lie down. He ran his hand down her back instead, so incredibly grateful she was in his arms, that she hadn't been lost to him forever.

It was easiest to lift her, bridal style, and put her down on the bed. He hadn't taken down the covers, but he managed to tuck her safely inside after a bit of maneuvering.

He watched her the whole time he undressed. She was out, completely still, even her breathing hidden below the comforter. But a single strand of her hair had broken free from the rest, and with every exhale, it quivered, making it hard to look anywhere else. It was proof enough until he could feel her again.

He didn't bother with shorts or pajama bottoms. He wanted to feel every part of her he could. When he climbed in to join her, he turned off the light, then pulled her close. Her head rested on his chest, her hand on his stomach. He wanted to kiss her, but she needed to sleep. So did he.

Just before he nodded off, she snuggled closer, one of her legs curling over his. He breathed easy for the first time since the ten o'clock news.

WHEN SHANNON OPENED HER eyes, the room was so full of light she had to squint. She was plastered against Nate, which was wonderful until the next second when she remembered what had happened at the TV studio. Her whole body seized in a clench and she closed her eyes so tightly she saw stars, but it didn't help. There was no magic that could change the past. She couldn't even hide in bed. The world had kept turning. They'd all been up so late. Had Brady opened up the plant? The company still had orders to fill. The employees still had jobs. All of them, including Daphne.

Shannon couldn't think about her, not yet. Nate was asleep. She moved carefully, trying not to wake him as she got out of bed. She didn't remember getting undressed. She donned her robe, her glance catching the clock. It was past noon. God, what havoc was waiting for her downstairs? In the real world.

She hurried in the bathroom so she could get back to Nate. She remembered him surprising her in front of the house, remembered his words and hoped like she'd never hoped that he meant them.

She brushed a lock of hair from his forehead, her heart aching for what she'd done, how she'd messed up so thoroughly. No one was that forgiving, not in the light of day. He'd been all over the news, and if last night hadn't been a horrible nightmare, his picture was now on the internet, as well. She doubted his bosses would be very thrilled about his notoriety.

She turned to get dressed but gasped as her wrist was caught by a strong hand.

"Where are you going?" he asked, his voice filled with sleep.

"To put on clothes. The second-worst day of my life begins."

He shook his head. "No. You're coming back to bed."

"I already thought of that, but I can't stay there forever. I'll have to face the music eventually."

"The music will wait for an hour." He let her go in order to sit up, but his gaze kept her right where she stood. "Please. I'm going down the hall for two minutes. Please be back in bed when I return."

"Nate—"

"For me."

She couldn't say no. In truth, she didn't want to. "Hurry," she said.

He was up more quickly than she'd have thought possible, his robe thrown on, and he was out the door. She was left in her too-bright room, the room of her childhood. The safest place on earth for most of her life. There would be no more procrastinating. She would find a place to move and leave this house. No matter what happened out there, whatever price she had to pay, she needed to step away from this cocoon. Maybe she'd have thought twice about her actions if she hadn't felt so protected all the time.

For now, though, she'd take the comfort. She let her robe drop where she was and crawled back under the sheets. She pulled her pillow close and breathed in the scent of Nate, so masculine and so him. She knew why his specific odor made her clench and shudder. She'd bonded with him. His scent would continue to please her for as long as they were together. Which wouldn't be long at all.

She inhaled again, not foolish enough to waste the good things she had. Not naive enough to believe she would get over him, not now. He would be the one man, the lost love. She would miss him forever, and even if eventually she did find someone else, Nate would remain the true love of her life.

She didn't mind. He was worth it.

It dawned on her that she was assuming that he'd wanted her to stay in bed to comfort her. It was equally likely he wanted the time to ask her what she'd been thinking. Why she'd lied. Why she'd ever thought it was all right to pass him around like a toy.

The door opened, and she tried to see it in his face, what he thought, what he wanted. His reason.

He dropped his robe, climbed in next to her and wrapped himself around her, kissing her as if it were the most important thing he'd ever do.

Thank God.

He tasted too much like mint, but that was okay. The bad things were coming, they were, but not while Nate kissed her. While he ran his hand down her back and up her arm, when he moved his thigh between her legs just hard enough to make her gasp. He kept surprising her. He should be angry. Maybe he was angry, but it didn't feel like that. His touch was too tender and his body too warm.

She didn't exactly trust her judgment, however, and this was important. "I know I told you this last night," she said, her lips an inch from his. She wasn't allowed to touch them again until she found out the score. Until she told him again. "But I need to say it one more time. A hundred times. I'm sorry. I'm so sorry that I used you, that my actions caused you to be embarrassed."

"Who says I'm embarrassed?"

"You're on a trading card. A trading card that trades men."

"I've always wanted to be on a trading card. I think I looked pretty good. Besides, you stole my card. I'm not sure, but I'm guessing you broke all kinds of trading card rules by your thievery. You need to apologize to the other ladies."

She laughed. She could hardly believe it was possible to laugh, or to feel this way about anyone. Ever. She'd had no idea what love was like, and now she did. Nothing else like it in the world. It felt as if…but no, her actual beating heart was changed because she loved

Nate Brenner. To love him with all her heart was a reality, not a poem. She wanted to tell him, she did, but because she loved him in such a real way, she wouldn't. He was leaving. He had another life, a world away. It wouldn't be fair, and he'd feel badly about it, and she would never want that for the man she loved.

"I'm glad you're not angry," she said.

He kissed her, a small kiss, just lips on lips, then pulled back far enough so that she could see his expression. "It would have been better to have asked because there might be men on the cards who would mind. I can't imagine it, but it's possible. But I'm not angry. I know you would never do anything to purposefully hurt anyone, especially not someone you care about. I know that you wanted your friends to be happy. To have fairy-tale lives and bigger-than-life love stories. How could I be angry about that?"

She was glad she'd been able to watch him through that speech. He meant every word. She didn't have to worry about Nate. Not a bit. "Okay," she said.

"You do know the rest is all going to work out, don't you?"

"Eventually."

"Sooner than you think," he said, right before he captured her mouth in another searing kiss. His hands went to the sides of her face to hold her steady as their kiss went from hot to torrid.

She wouldn't have minded if that's all they'd done. Yes, she was aching with want, and yes, every time he rubbed his chest against hers it sent shivers all through her body. She pressed against his thigh, riding him, and it was almost as good as being filled, of being as close as they could possibly be. And then it wasn't enough.

"More," she whispered. "Please."

Tearing himself away, he rolled over, grabbed a condom and was back before she finished her exhale. "More. Yes. Everything. God, I want you." His hiss told her he was ready, and she grabbed the pillow she wasn't using, placing it in the general area of her hips before she lay back.

He moaned as he followed her, kissing whatever part of her he could—the inside of her elbow, her nipple, the side of her neck. Random sizzling sparks all over, everywhere his lips and tongue landed.

When he was above her, braced on his arms, she could see his desire for her in his dark eyes. Even when the lights had been on at night, she'd never seen so much of him. The crazy sleep hair that made him look adorable. He'd shaved, of course she'd known that somewhere because she hadn't felt his beard, but he'd had to have shaved *fast* because he hadn't been gone long. Lucky thing he hadn't cut himself. She touched his jaw, his chin, making sure. All she felt was smooth, warm skin. When he dipped down and captured her finger in his mouth, she gasped again. He was so good at that.

She spread her legs for him. "Please," she said again. "Come inside me. Fill me up. Make me forget about everything but you."

He pushed into her slowly, his gaze unwavering. "Oh, Christ, how you scared me. When I thought I'd never see you again, I couldn't think what to do." His eyes clenched as he seated himself all the way. Both of them were breathing harder now, faster, their chests rising and falling in perfect synchrony. "Promise me you'll never run like that again." He pulled out and pushed back in. "Promise."

She wanted to tell him she wasn't the one who was

running away. Instead she ran her hands down his back and looked him straight in the eyes. "I promise I will never run from you. Ever."

17

NATE STARED AS STRANDS OF Shannon's silky hair slipped through his fingers to fall on the pillow. She was dozing, still tired after such a grueling night, and then they'd made love. His gaze went from her hair to her face. Her eyelashes were red. Red. He should have noticed that by now. Maybe she wore dark mascara on them, because how could he have missed the wonder of her red lashes?

He didn't know what to do. She'd suffered last night, and even if everyone in the city told her she was forgiven, he doubted she would believe it. Not until she'd made the amends she felt she must. After that? She was sensible, she'd go on with her life, but the memory would always hurt her.

He couldn't add to that. He didn't want to be part of anything that would always hurt Shannon. That was unacceptable, and even though it would be turning his back on the family who'd loved him best, he had to tell them that he wouldn't help. He'd rather cut off his own arm.

The air slipped out of his lungs as reality hit him anew. He had fallen in love. The impossible thing had happened. He was no longer the same man. Shannon had changed everything.

He got out of bed, and when he heard her squeak as she stretched, he smiled at her. "I was going to go shower. But I can wait if you'd like to go first."

When she shook her head, she looked at him as if nothing were wrong, as if last night had never happened. "Go ahead. But you'd better not use all the hot water."

He tightened his robe, then kissed her softly. "I won't be long."

"Good."

As he walked down the hall, the ripples of his new awareness started expanding. At the center was Shannon. Everything flowed from there. He had decisions to make.

SHANNON HAD DRESSED FOR work, although she doubted she would make it to the plant. It was almost two o'clock, and she was about to face her family.

Nate was right behind her as she walked down the stairs. They both stopped at the living room entrance. "You're all here."

"Brady's at the plant," her dad said. "Paula and Alice have gone to work."

She wasn't sure what it meant, that they'd stayed. Support? An intervention? "I hope there's some coffee."

"Danny, go get them some coffee," her mother said.

Danny didn't even make a fuss.

Shannon was growing more concerned by the moment. Her mom was wearing one of her company dresses. Not going-out-to-the-theater nice, but a cut above the norm.

"There's been a number of phone calls this morning," her father said.

Shannon winced. "Sorry. I'll certainly be saying that a lot today."

Danny came back with two mugs and put them on the coffee table. Coincidentally, there were two seats open on the couch. Shannon and Nate went to sit down, although her stomach was so tense she couldn't even think of drinking at the moment.

"I don't see why you should have to apologize," her mom said. "On the other hand, that reporter fellow needs to be tarred and feathered."

Nate threaded his fingers between hers where they lay on the couch.

"Well, I think what happened last night was a good thing," Danny said. "We all needed a little shaking up."

"What?" Shannon asked, appalled. "What part of that horror show was good?"

"For one thing, Fitzgerald and Sons is getting a lot of publicity."

"That's not the sort of publicity we want."

"Depends on what the objective is, doesn't it?" Danny gave her a lopsided smile.

Shannon leaned forward, wondering if she were still asleep and having one hell of a weird dream. "What are you talking about?"

Looks were exchanged. None of them with her. Nate scooted closer to her.

"First of all," her mother said, "we love you, and we have no quarrels with you using the plant for your own projects. It's your company, too."

"And?" Shannon said, her voice quivering.

"And we all agree you've done a wonderful job at the

plant. We would have closed a long time ago if it wasn't for your efforts."

"We appreciate that," her dad said. "I'm being a hundred-percent honest here. Every one of us knows you've worked yourself to the bone keeping us in business."

"But," Myles said, "we think that the days of Fitzgerald and Sons are over."

Shannon felt as though she'd been punched in the gut. If it wasn't for Nate's steady arm slipping around her, she'd have crumpled into a tiny ball. "Oh, God. I've ruined everything. I knew it was bad. I didn't think—"

"Wait, wait. You didn't ruin anything." Her mother came closer, sat down across from Shannon. "Sweetheart, listen to me. This isn't your doing. The truth is your father and I are getting on in years. We're tired of worrying about that old plant. We've been talking about retiring."

"In Florida," Danny said. "Tell her, Ma."

"That's right. We're also very tired of the snow. If I never see another flake…"

"You've been talking about it?" Shannon asked. "For how long?"

Her mother took in a deep breath. "For a while, Shannon. A while."

"The land's worth a fortune," Danny added, and damn him, he sounded excited. "That's prime territory. We're talking millions."

She could barely believe what she was hearing. They wanted to sell the plant. Move to Florida. Retire. She looked at every single member of her family, and each one was looking more abashed then the next. Except for Danny, of course. "Why didn't you say anything?"

"Because you were working so hard," her mother

said. "Although, to give us some credit, you do realize I've been telling you for years that you should find your own dreams."

"I thought you were talking about a husband."

The doorbell rang, and her brothers all made a dash out of the room as if it were a fire drill.

Shannon turned to look at Nate, and he seemed just as disconcerted as her folks. "Did you know about this?"

He nodded.

She pulled her hand free, feeling gut-shot. "How could you…?"

"I didn't want to tell you even though you needed to know. I'm sorry. I thought I was doing you a favor waiting until you'd had your interview."

"But why did you know before me?"

He winced, then took hold of her hand again. "Because your family loves you, and no one wanted to hurt you. They thought it would be kinder coming from me."

"I see."

"They didn't know I couldn't go through with it. I couldn't. I also know that you deserve a chance to find out who you want to be. You're amazing, Shannon. You can be anything you want."

"I thought I wanted to keep my family together," she said.

"Sweetheart," her mother said, looking right into her eyes, "we're still going to be a family. That will never change. No matter where we live, or where we work."

"Shannon." Tim motioned with his chin. "You've got some people here."

Dizzy with too much information, she rose on shaky feet. Nate got up, too, and together they went toward the foyer.

Shannon stopped when she saw Rebecca and Bree, along with Katy and her cousin Ariel standing inside the door. As if she hadn't had enough battering for the day. "I was going to call all of you," she said. "I'm so, so sorry."

"For what?" Rebecca asked.

"For putting you in such a horrible position. Everyone from the lunch exchange."

The women approached, none of them looking as if they'd been crying, or even upset. "There's been a lot of explaining," Bree said. "But no one's mad."

"Jake said he was flattered as hell. Grateful to you for getting us together."

"We've been on the phone all morning," Katy said. "Letting the cat out of the bag, so to speak. So far, everyone's been cool about it."

Shannon turned to Bree. "Charlie?"

"He's fine." Bree shrugged. "Quite amused, in fact."

"He's more than fine," Rebecca said. "Between his attorneys and mine, we will own that TV station. There's going to be a press conference tomorrow morning where Grant Yost is going to make a very public apology. You're going to be famous, but for all the right reasons. The trading cards are brilliant. Whether the men are in on the game or not."

Danny popped up between Nate and Ariel. "Brady's on the phone," he said, speaking to Shannon. "He needs to speak to you. Now."

She took the phone, wondering what bombshell Brady was going to drop.

"Shannon?"

"What's going on?"

"The phones are going crazy. I haven't had a second to do anything else. People are insane."

"What people?"

"Women. Men. From all over the damn country. First it was local, then it started spreading west."

"Excuse me?"

"They want the trading cards. Women want to start their own clubs and men want to be on the cards. It's nuts."

Shannon pulled the phone away from her ear and looked at it, sure there must be something wrong with it. "He says people are calling. To do their own trading cards. Women. Men."

Nate helped her bring the phone back to her ear. Brady was saying something she didn't catch. "What was that?"

"Not just the trading cards," he said. "But that literary publishing house in SoHo?"

"Yeah?"

"They want us to be their printer."

"I called them weeks ago."

"They're not the only ones. We've had three new orders placed, all from your cold calls."

It was too much. Shannon couldn't take in anymore. She handed the phone to Nate as tears filled her eyes. That wouldn't have been so bad if she weren't having so much trouble breathing.

"Shannon." Ariel came over and hugged her. "What's wrong? This is good news, isn't it? That everyone can see what a great idea you had? How many people you've made happy?"

Shannon nodded, but she couldn't speak. She couldn't stop crying, either. Then she was being shifted from one pair of arms to another—to the right pair. Nate held her close and tight, rocking her gently. "It's going to be okay, sweetie. You'll see. It's just overwhelming right now. Breathe, okay?"

"The only thing is," Rebecca said, "we can't figure out how WNYC found out about the trading cards. No one in the group would want this. We were all enjoying it too much."

Shannon sniffed, wiped at her face as she stepped away from Nate. "It wasn't anyone in the group. I'm pretty sure it was someone at the plant."

"Who?" Danny's eyes blazed.

"Never mind that," she said. "I'll take care of it."

"I hope whoever it is will be happy on unemployment."

"Danny, you don't know the situation. You're always so quick on the trigger."

"You okay?" Nate asked.

"I will be. Once I sort things out. I don't understand half of what's going on."

"Right. Executive decision." He looked at the women in front of him and the family behind. "I'm taking Shannon away for the night. For two nights, in fact. We're going to pack her a bag, and then we're leaving. She needs time to think, and so do you all. We'll see you again at the Easter egg hunt, where I expect all of you to donate as much as possible."

Shannon stared up at him. "But—"

"We need to talk. I have some calls to make, which I'll do while you're packing your bag. Make sure you've got your Sunday things with you. Now go on upstairs. I'll be with you as soon as I can."

She sniffed again and smiled. "Sounds like a plan."

Then he kissed her. Right in front of everybody.

THE FIRST THING HE DID WHEN he got Shannon inside their room at the Gramercy Park Hotel was order dinner. Nate knew she'd barely eaten a thing, and that the past twenty-four hours had turned her world upside down.

He also knew he was going to be adding yet another layer of improbable to the mix.

They'd ordered nothing more extravagant than pasta and salad with a good bottle of red wine. He liked the idea that they were staying at the hotel where they'd first danced together. That so much had happened since that wedding was difficult to believe, but he was used to that. It was a wild ride, this life, and things happened at breakneck speed. The trick was to be holding on to the reins, not the tail.

His poor Shannon wasn't quite in saddle yet. She hadn't spoken much, but he could see by her eyes that she was sorting and sifting and working hard to get her bearings. He was ready to help, but he needed her more stable before he got to the main event.

Luckily, room service had believed him about the extra tip, and he made good on his promise when the food arrived. The waiter set them up on the table in the room, the pasta steaming hot, the salad crisp and the wine excellent.

For the first ten minutes or so, there was just eating. Getting the hunger under control had been vital, and now that they were both slowing down, he felt ready to begin.

"So, I've made a couple of changes to my itinerary," he said.

"Don't tell me you have to leave sooner than you'd planned."

He shouldn't have started off so glibly. Shannon looked as though one more blow would do her in. "No, I'm not. In fact, I'm not leaving at all."

Her fork clattered on her plate. "What? What does that mean?"

He reached over and put his hand on top of hers. "It

means I'm not going back to Bali. Or going to Africa. Well, okay, I'll have to go to Bali to get my things, but I'm hoping you'll come with me, because you really need a vacation after this week."

Shannon stared at him, her lips parted, her eyebrows raised in a perfect picture of shocked surprise. "That makes no sense."

"Why not?"

"You love your job. Your work is everything to you."

"Not…quite," he said. Then he picked up his glass of wine and held it as if in a toast. "Turns out, you're everything to me."

That didn't make her any less shocked. In fact, he wondered if she should be worried about how pale she looked. "Shannon?"

"Did you just say…?"

"Yeah. I'm staying here, in New York. In the co-op I just bought. And I'm hoping you'll consider moving into that co-op with me. When we've finished furnishing the place."

"What about…everything?"

"I've decided there's my kind of work to be done right here in the city. I'm going to buy out Albert Gill's half of the business. We're still going to make fast-food franchise buildings and ugly strip malls, but I'm also going to repurpose our business plan to include restoration and rebuilding of community areas, starting with a certain corner basketball court. If the owners let us, that is. Anyway, I'm an urban planner and architect, and New York needs my kind of people. So I'm staying."

Shannon's mouth opened, then closed. Then she leaned forward. "You mentioned living together?"

"Right. That's kind of key to the whole deal. See, I've fallen in love with you. I didn't expect to, but you are just the most remarkable woman I've ever met, and the idea of leaving you doesn't work for me anymore. I want to start a new life here, Shannon. With you. I'd like for you to consider working on the nonprofit side of the new firm. Only if you want to. I still think you'd be fantastic on the city council, but more than that, you should find out what you want. I hope that what you want includes me."

"You've fallen in love with me."

He hadn't seen her blink in a while. "Yeah. Pretty hard, to be honest."

"Oh. I…"

"Shannon? You okay?"

She blinked. And then she smiled. And it was one hell of a smile. "I've fallen in love with you, too."

"Thank God." He put his wine down, then went over to where Shannon was sitting. He leaned over and kissed her. Then he kissed her again. "This is a whole new beginning."

"We can start our own legacy," she whispered, her eyes moist and sparkling.

He brushed the back of his fingers across her pale cheek. "It's going to be fantastic. Even the scary parts."

She laughed. Then she stood up, and they kissed some more.

BY THE TIME THEY GOT TO THE park on Sunday, Shannon had gotten a lot of things straightened out in her head. She had personal apologies yet to make, and no matter how many of her friends from the lunch exchange said it wasn't necessary, she would be in touch with every single trading card man.

She'd gotten on a speaker call with the family, who'd made a few decisions of their own. They weren't going to sell the plant after all. Brady wanted to stay, and there were so many new orders and so much interest in the trading cards that they were going to hold off. See what happened. But they were going to have to find themselves a new Shannon. Because after she'd helped train whomever they hired, she was going to be busy.

Moving out of the brownstone was going to be a huge undertaking. For everyone. Her parents would be heading off to sunny Florida. Brady was moving in with Paula. And she was heading to a brand-new life with Nate.

The booths were all set up, the Easter baskets looked terrific on the beautiful April day and her whole clan was already in position. Little kids were arriving in their Sunday best, Easter bonnets were everywhere and the sound of laughter rippled in the breeze.

When Shannon tried to get behind the counter to take donations, she was summarily dismissed by one of her mother's book-club friends. In fact, Shannon wasn't needed anywhere. Friends from the lunch exchange, from the neighborhood, the church, business contacts… it felt as if everyone she'd ever met was in the park that afternoon, and they all wanted to speak to her about the trading cards, about that horrible Grant Yost and how he was so apologetic on the news. And on the internet. And on every other local New York TV station.

It was all pretty glorious. But the best part was the man with his arm around her shoulders. The man she'd fallen head over heels in love with.

The man whose trading card was still in her purse.

* * * * *

PASSION

Harlequin® Blaze

COMING NEXT MONTH
AVAILABLE APRIL 24, 2012

#681 NOT JUST FRIENDS
The Wrong Bed
Kate Hoffmann

#682 COMING UP FOR AIR
Uniformly Hot!
Karen Foley

#683 NORTHERN FIRES
Alaskan Heat
Jennifer LaBrecque

#684 HER MAN ADVANTAGE
Double Overtime
Joanne Rock

#685 SIZZLE IN THE CITY
Flirting with Justice
Wendy Etherington

#686 BRINGING HOME A BACHELOR
All the Groom's Men
Karen Kendall

REQUEST YOUR FREE BOOKS!
2 FREE NOVELS PLUS 2 FREE GIFTS!

Harlequin *Blaze*

r e d - h o t r e a d s !

YES! Please send me 2 FREE Harlequin® Blaze™ novels and my 2 FREE gifts (gifts are worth about $10). After receiving them, if I don't wish to receive any more books, I can return the shipping statement marked "cancel." If I don't cancel, I will receive 6 brand-new novels every month and be billed just $4.49 per book in the U.S. or $4.96 per book in Canada. That's a saving of at least 14% off the cover price. It's quite a bargain. Shipping and handling is just 50¢ per book in the U.S. and 75¢ per book in Canada.* I understand that accepting the 2 free books and gifts places me under no obligation to buy anything. I can always return a shipment and cancel at any time. Even if I never buy another book, the two free books and gifts are mine to keep forever.

151/351 HDN FEQE

Name	(PLEASE PRINT)
Address	Apt. #
City	State/Prov.	Zip/Postal Code

Signature (if under 18, a parent or guardian must sign)

Mail to the **Reader Service:**
IN U.S.A.: P.O. Box 1867, Buffalo, NY 14240-1867
IN CANADA: P.O. Box 609, Fort Erie, Ontario L2A 5X3

Not valid for current subscribers to Harlequin Blaze books.

Want to try two free books from another line?
Call 1-800-873-8635 or visit www.ReaderService.com.

* Terms and prices subject to change without notice. Prices do not include applicable taxes. Sales tax applicable in N.Y. Canadian residents will be charged applicable taxes. Offer not valid in Quebec. This offer is limited to one order per household. All orders subject to credit approval. Credit or debit balances in a customer's account(s) may be offset by any other outstanding balance owed by or to the customer. Please allow 4 to 6 weeks for delivery. Offer available while quantities last.

Your Privacy—The Reader Service is committed to protecting your privacy. Our Privacy Policy is available online at www.ReaderService.com or upon request from the Reader Service.

We make a portion of our mailing list available to reputable third parties that offer products we believe may interest you. If you prefer that we not exchange your name with third parties, or if you wish to clarify or modify your communication preferences, please visit us at www.ReaderService.com/consumerchoice or write to us at Reader Service Preference Service, P.O. Box 9062, Buffalo, NY 14269. Include your complete name and address.

HBI IB

Julia McKee and Adam Sutherland never got along in college, but somehow, several years after graduation, they got stuck sharing the same bed on a weekend getaway with mutual friends. Can this very wrong bed suddenly make everything right between them?

Read on for a sneak peek from
NOT JUST FRIENDS by Kate Hoffmann.

Available May 2012, only from Harlequin® Blaze™.

"DO YOU REMEMBER the day we met?" Julia asked.

Adam groaned. "Oh, God, don't remind me. It was not my finest moment. My mind and my mouth were temporarily disengaged. I'd hoped you'd find me charming, but somehow, I don't think that was the case." He took her hand and pressed a kiss to her wrist, staring up at her with a teasing glint in his eyes.

Julia's gaze fixed on the spot where his lips warmed her skin. "Does that usually work on women?" she asked. "A little kiss on the wrist? And then the puppy-dog eyes?"

His smile faded. "You think I'm just playing you?"

"I've considered it," Julia said. But now that she saw the hurt expression on his face, she realized she'd been wrong.

She drew a deep breath and smiled. "I'm starving. Are you hungry?" Julia hopped out of bed, then grabbed his hand and pulled him up. "I can make us something to eat."

They wandered out to the kitchen, her hand still clasped in his, and when they reached the refrigerator, she pulled the door open and peered inside.

Grabbing a carton of eggs, she turned to face him. His hands were braced on either side of her body, holding the door open. Julia felt a shiver skitter over her skin.

Slowly, Adam bent toward her, touching his lips to hers. Julia had been kissed by her fair share of men, but it had never felt like this. Maybe it was the refrigerator sending cold air across her back. Or maybe it was just all the years that had passed between them and all the chances they'd avoided because of one silly slight on the day they'd met.

He drew back, then ran his hand over her cheek and smiled. "I've wanted to do that for eight years," he said.

Julia swallowed hard. "Eight?"

He nodded. "Since the moment I met you, Jules."

Find out what happens in NOT JUST FRIENDS
by Kate Hoffmann.

Available May 2012, only from Harlequin® Blaze™.

HBEXP0412